DANNY DANGER

and the
COSMIC REMOTE

ADAM FROST

nosy
Crow

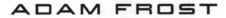

To Anna and Eliza

First published in the UK in 2011 by Nosy Crow Ltd
The Crow's Nest, 11 The Chandlery
50 Westminster Bridge Road
London, SE1 7QY, UK

www.nosycrow.com

Nosy Crow and associated logos are trademarks and/or
registered trademarks of Nosy Crow Ltd

Text © Adam Frost, 2011
Illustrations © Andy Parker, 2011

The right of Adam Frost and Andy Parker to be identified as the author
and illustrator respectively of this work has been asserted by them in accordance
with the Copyright, Designs and Patents Act, 1988

1 3 5 7 9 10 8 6 4 2

Printed and bound in the UK by
Clays Ltd, St Ives Plc

Papers used by Nosy Crow are made from wood grown in sustainable forests

ISBN: 978 0 857 63017 9

1
PLAY

It was a Monday afternoon and Danny Danger was sitting quietly in a maths lesson, holding his cosmic remote control.

Nobody else in the class could see it, because he held it flat against his leg, ready to slip it back into his pocket at any time.

It was about half of the size of a normal remote with just seven buttons: On/Off, Play, Pause, Stop, Record, Fast Forward and Rewind. Above the buttons, there was a small LCD showing the current time: **10:16:53.**

Instead of a battery compartment, there was a small amber crystal embedded in the back, which rotated slowly when the remote was active, glinting and sparkling and shimmering as it turned.

The teacher stood at the front of the class, pointing to an equation on the whiteboard. His name was Mr Boswell. He had a big orange nose with three thick black bristles sticking out of each nostril. He wore thick square glasses that made his eyes look like tiny dots, although when he took his glasses off to mop his forehead, then his eyes were suddenly as big as fruit bowls. He was completely bald except for three long crinkled hairs that looked like they'd been drawn on his head with a biro.

Mr Boswell was explaining how three fours were the same as four threes, and that three times three times four was the same as four times three times three.

Danny stifled a yawn and his eyes swam. He looked round at his classmates, slumped forwards on their desks or staring vacantly out of the window. Mr Boswell jabbed the air with a marker pen while his other hand jingled loose change in his pocket. Danny's thumb hovered over his cosmic remote and he pressed Fast Forward.

Mr Boswell's lips started moving very quickly and he scribbled on the board, then talked, then scribbled on the board five times faster than he normally would have done. His face suddenly turned red and sweaty as he lost his temper, then very quickly faded back to white again. The numbers on Danny's remote spun round rapidly; the seconds were almost too quick to see - 56 57 58 59 -

as 10:18

became 10:19

and then 10:20.

Outside birds whipped past like bullets; clouds tumbled by like clothes in a washing machine.

One of Danny's friends whizzed out of the classroom to go to the toilet, then whizzed back in again and sat down.

At that moment, Mr Boswell's head snapped round. He was staring at Danny; he was speeding towards him with a furious expression on his face.

Danny let go of Fast Forward and for a split second Mr Boswell was shouting: "Daniel Danger, I won't ask you again—"

Then Danny pressed Rewind and Mr Boswell walked backwards, stopped by the board and turned to face the class again.

Danny let go of Rewind and life resumed its normal speed.

"So let's find out who's been paying attention, shall we?" Mr Boswell was saying. "Daniel Danger, you've been very quiet. Why don't we start with you?"

Danny blinked and looked down at his desk.

"Today we've been learning about multiplication, haven't we?' said Mr Boswell. "So I'm sure you'll be able to tell me what five times five times five comes to. That's right. Five times five times five."

Danny tried to form the numbers in his head. Five lots of five – five times. Fifty-five?

Mr Boswell was walking towards Danny. "Daniel Danger, I won't ask you again," he huffed. "Five times five times five."

Danny imagined writing the numbers down, but he was distracted by the stains on Mr Boswell's tie and the hair on Mr Boswell's ears and Mr Boswell's smelly breath and Mr Boswell's wobbly double chin.

"Daniel Danger!" roared Mr Boswell. "You haven't listened to a single word I've said."

Danny looked up at Mr Boswell's bright-red face. He took a deep breath and pressed Pause on his cosmic remote. The crystal started to spin round and the time display flashed:

10:34... 10:34... 10:34...

Everything had frozen. Mr Boswell's mouth was half open, his eyebrows were raised and his hands were hanging in mid-air.

Danny's classmates were still and silent. Some had been whispering, some had been scribbling in their exercise books, some had been scowling at Mr Boswell; now they were all as motionless as statues, unable to blink or breathe or move a muscle.

Danny stood up and walked out of the classroom.

Out in the corridor he saw Mrs Jenkins, the deputy head, frozen in mid-stride. She had a bundle of papers under her right arm and a mobile phone in her left. She had just sneezed so she had a funny expression on her face: eyes closed, cheeks puffed out and a shower of spit hovering in front of her nose.

Danny squeezed past her and walked through the entrance hall towards the library.

Outside on the school field Mr Chambers's class had been halfway through a game of rounders. The ball was suspended two metres above the ground; one of the boys was halfway between second and third base; one of the girls was standing underneath the ball, steeling herself for a catch. Danny really wanted to press Play on his cosmic remote and see whether the boy would get his rounder, but he knew this would be a big mistake. He would suddenly vanish from Mr Boswell's class, right in front of everyone's eyes, and how would he explain that?

He pushed open the door of the library and walked inside.

It was completely empty except for the school cat, sleeping on a stool in a shaft of sunlight. Danny stroked the cat but she was as stiff as a board and didn't purr and nuzzle his hand as she normally did.

Danny spotted the cupboard he was looking for and walked towards it. He closed his eyes as he went to open it, thinking it would be locked, but the door swung open, and he breathed a sigh of relief.

Inside there were rows of red boxes labelled DIGITAL CAMERA, MP3 PLAYERS, HEADPHONES and BLANK CDs. A loudhailer sat on top of a DVD player. On the bottom shelf he saw a box labelled CALCULATORS, which he slid out. He grabbed a calculator from the pile and typed in 5 x 5 x 5. The answer was 125.

He whispered to himself, "One hundred and twenty-five, one hundred and twenty-five, one hundred and twenty-five," until he was sure he remembered it.

He tossed the calculator back in the box, closed the cupboard door and walked quickly out of the library.

He ran back to his classroom, glancing down at the cosmic remote.

The time was still flashing: **10:34.**

He looked up just in time to see Mrs Jenkins. He swerved to avoid her but knocked the mobile phone out of her hand. It hit the floor and the back spun off. He fiddled with the phone for a few seconds until the back snapped into place again. Then he settled the phone back in her hand at what he hoped was the right angle.

He rushed back into his classroom and sat back in his chair, staring up at Mr Boswell's angry, menacing face. He pressed Play on his cosmic remote and everything came back to life.

"One hundred and twenty-five," said Danny.

"What?" barked Mr Boswell.

"One hundred and twenty-five. That's the answer," said Danny.

"The answer to what?" spluttered Mr Boswell.

"The sum. The sum you just gave me," explained Danny.

Mr Boswell started to speak, then stopped, then frowned, then stared at Danny.

"Hmph," he said.

The rest of the class began to whisper and titter.

"Silence!" shouted Mr Boswell and looked at Danny suspiciously again.

That afternoon Danny walked home with his best friend, Eric Taylor. Eric was in a different class with a different teacher.

"How was Headcase?" asked Eric.

Headcase was their nickname for Mr Boswell.

"Same as usual. How was Stinkbomb?" asked Danny.

Stinkbomb was their nickname for Eric's teacher, Miss Beecham. She had nine cats and her clothes smelled a bit funny.

"Same as usual," said Eric. "Are you coming round later?"

"Don't know," said Danny. "Mum and Dad aren't letting me do anything at the moment."

"That's a pain," said Eric. "I got a new computer game off my Uncle Steve. Zombie

Goblins II. In level 2, you can teleport and in level 3, you can become invisible. You've got to have a go!"

"That sounds great!" said Danny.

Eric didn't know about Danny's cosmic remote – nobody did. Danny had come close to telling Eric a few times because he knew how amazed and excited Eric would have been. But when he'd got the remote, he'd been warned to tell no one about it – unless there was an emergency. Today had been a bit of a drag, but not an emergency.

Danny turned into the street where they both lived.

"So I might see you later on," said Eric.

"Fingers crossed," replied Danny.

Eric walked up his driveway and Danny crossed the road and headed for his house. He went through the side gate and opened the back door.

The kitchen seemed to be empty. It was a fairly big kitchen with lots of cupboards and a long dining table at one end of it.

On every wall of the house, there were tea towels in frames with helpful mottos stitched on to them. In the kitchen, there was one hanging above the sink.

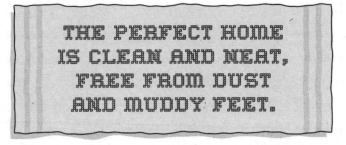

THE PERFECT HOME
IS CLEAN AND NEAT,
FREE FROM DUST
AND MUDDY FEET.

There was another tea towel above the washing machine.

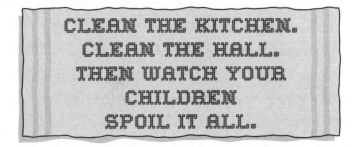

CLEAN THE KITCHEN.
CLEAN THE HALL.
THEN WATCH YOUR
CHILDREN
SPOIL IT ALL.

Danny breathed a deep sigh, relieved that nobody else seemed to be home.

Then Danny's mum and dad walked into the

kitchen, side by side. His big sister, Mia, was a few paces behind them, looking pleased with herself. Danny's hand dived into his pocket and his thumb hovered over the Rewind button on his cosmic remote.

Mrs Danger had a long thin face that was always red with anger. Mr Danger's face was big and round like the moon with a wisp of grey hair on top like smoke coming out of a chimney. Danny's sister Mia looked a bit like Danny, only her hair was long and straight and blonde rather than short and tufty and brown.

"Daniel Patrick Danger," declared Mrs Danger. "Your father would like a word with you."

"I certainly would," said Mr Danger. "Tell him, darling."

"Your father would like to know why you haven't tidied your room," said Mrs Danger.

"I did tidy my room!" Danny protested.

"Moving everything into a big heap in the middle of the room isn't the same as tidying," squeaked Mrs Danger.

"Isn't it?" said Danny. "Why not?"

"Your father has explained this to you many times," said Mrs Danger. "Drawers not floors. Clean it like you mean it."

"I definitely said that," said Mr Danger. "I remember it very clearly."

Mia's head poked out from behind her father and she smirked.

Mrs Danger let out a whoop of grief.

"Are those grass stains on your elbows?" she exclaimed. "I don't believe it! Hector, look at this!"

Mr Danger bent over and squinted at Danny's shirt.

"Well, that's coming out of your pocket money," growled Mr Danger.

"And is that a rip in your trousers?" spluttered Mrs Danger.

Mr Danger leaned in again.

"That's coming out of your pocket money too," he said.

"You don't give me any pocket money," protested Danny. "You never have!"

"Is it any wonder?" wailed Mrs Danger. "The amount we have to spend cleaning up after you!"

"Mum, I smell dog poo," said Mia. "I definitely smell dog poo."

Mrs Danger gasped and put a hand over her mouth. "And you've trodden it into the kitchen carpet!"

"That wasn't me!" cried Danny. He lifted up his left shoe and then his right shoe. There it was.

"Take them off! Take them off!" gibbered Mrs Danger.

Mia looked at Danny with a satisfied smile. Danny pulled his shoes off and they hit the floor with a thud.

"You're a disgrace to the Danger family name," growled Mr Danger. "You should act like a Danger to everyone you meet. That's what we all do!"

"Now, go to your room before you do any more damage!" moaned Mrs Danger.

Danny trudged slowly up the stairs, gripping his cosmic remote like a vice. He should press Pause and go back downstairs. He could slap his dad's belly and twist his sister's nose.

Or he could scrape the dog poo off his shoes and transfer it on to his mother's shoes. Then Rewind back to the moment when his sister smelled it. Then who'd have messed up the kitchen carpet?

But Danny had had enough of his family for one afternoon. He just wanted to spend some time alone in his room, then climb out of the window and head for Eric's house.

He walked across the spotless landing and past his parents' immaculate bedroom. He was nearly blinded by the glint of windows and mirrors and ornaments. He almost choked on the smell of air freshener and shoe polish and washing powder.

Ten seconds later, he was in his room with the door closed. His whole body relaxed. There were the clothes in a mound on the floor, the books dropped on the bed, the pens and rulers and notepads spread out on the desk, the comics scattered on the windowsill and radiator and bedside table. Danny smiled, leaned against the door and slid down on to the floor.

He thought about the evening ahead of him. If he was going to sneak over to Eric's, it made sense to use his cosmic remote. His parents had told him to stay in his room; if he disobeyed, they'd make his life even more miserable.

Danny placed the cosmic remote on the bed. He pointed it towards his desk and pressed Record. The crystal on the back turned red and started to spin round slowly. A cone of golden light shot out of the end of the remote and bathed the desk in a pale white glow. Danny stepped into the shaft of light and sat at the desk. He picked up a piece of paper and spent twenty minutes drawing a picture of a unicorn.

Then he reached over to a pile of comics that was balanced precariously on the edge of the desk. He pulled a comic out from halfway down the pile and spent three quarters of an hour reading it. That was enough, he thought to himself. He walked out of the shaft of light, picked up his cosmic remote and pressed Stop.

The crystal on the back of the remote began to flash red-orange red-orange. This meant that the recording had been successfully stored.

Danny looked at the time on the top of the remote: **6:01**.

Now would be a good time to go and see Eric.

Playing back a section of time was one of the best things about having a cosmic remote, Danny thought. He pointed the remote at the desk again and used his forefinger to press the crystal down until he heard a click. Then at the same time he pressed Play with his thumb. An image seemed to leap out of the end of the remote and settle at the desk. It was Danny, just as he had been an hour ago, drawing a picture of a unicorn. The image flickered, blurred and then came into focus.

The real Danny slipped the remote into his pocket and headed for the window. He looked at the recorded Danny sitting at the desk and gave it a big smile although he knew it would not be able to smile back.

Now if his parents checked up on him, there he would be, sitting quietly in his room, and that would be that; they'd leave him alone for another hour or so.

At **6:04** he was on the roof of Eric's extension, knocking on the window of Eric's bedroom.

His friend let him in.

"Cool, you made it," said Eric.

"I've only got about an hour," said Danny.

"How come?" asked Eric.

"Er ... my parents ... you know," stammered Danny.

Danny really wanted to tell Eric the truth. He could tell him, then press Rewind, and erase the whole conversation from time. But it seemed a bit pointless – and unfair on Eric.

"Shall we play on my computer?" exclaimed Eric. "Or I got this Build Your Own Robot kit from my Uncle Martin. I haven't opened it yet!"

"That sounds brilliant!" replied Danny.

Eric slid the robot kit out from under his bed and opened the box. Danny had never seen so many coils and springs and wires and computer

chips and bolts and plates of metal and light bulbs and pistons. It made him wonder what the inside of his cosmic remote looked like.

Danny started on the robot's right arm and Eric started on the left. You had to slot each finger into a small iron grid.

At one point, Eric's mum poked her head round the door.

"Hello, Danny, I didn't

know you were here," she said. "Do you boys want anything to eat?"

"Chocolate!" exclaimed Eric.

"Apart from chocolate," said Eric's mum, with a smile.

"Chocolate spread on toast?" tried Eric.

"How about peanut butter on toast?" replied Eric's mum.

"You're on!" declared Eric.

Eric's mum smiled and shook her head.

When the toast arrived, Danny and Eric were careful not to get any crumbs or blobs of peanut butter in the robot's components.

Then Danny looked up. "What's the time?"

Eric looked up too. "Don't know."

Danny quickly pulled out the edge of his cosmic remote and glanced at the time: **6:59**.

"Got to go," blurted out Danny.

He ran towards Eric's window.

"See you tomorrow at school," he said.

"But you left half your toast," protested Eric.

"You have it," said Danny, as he climbed on to the extension roof.

"Yesss!" whispered Eric.

The crystal in the cosmic remote was still glowing orange. This meant that the section of time was still playing; the pretend Danny was still sitting at his desk.

Danny crossed the road.

6:59 became 7:00.

He was in front of his house. He saw a light on in the living room. There was his father but where was his mother?

He trotted round the back of his house and shimmied up the drainpipe. On the way up he thought he saw the top of his mum's head crossing the landing window. She seemed to be heading for his room.

He got to the top of the drainpipe as fast as he could. He got one foot on the windowsill and then the other. He crouched down and slid into his room.

He could see the door handle being turned.

He could hear his mother's voice: "Daniel!"

He looked down at the cosmic remote:

7:02.

He looked at his desk: the other Danny was still sitting there reading.

His mind raced through all the possibilities. If he dived under the bed, his mother would only see one Danny – at the desk. He could run towards the door and stop his mother coming in – then she'd never see the Danny at the desk. He could pull out his cosmic remote and press Stop, but it always took about five seconds for the image to fade away completely and, besides, then his mother would see the cosmic remote and ask what it was.

But now the door was open and his mother was standing there.

7:02 became **7:03.**

The image of Danny at the desk began to fizzle out. For a split second, Mrs Danger saw two

Dannys – one at the desk and one by the window. She blinked twice. She reached down for the glasses hanging round her neck and put them on.

"That's better," she said.

Only one Danny remained.

"Your father has come to a decision," she began. "Tomorrow he is going to hire a skip. And everything in your room is going in it. All your comics, all your toys. Until you start treating our possessions with respect, we won't be respecting yours!"

She nodded curtly – as if to say "Serves you right!" – and closed the door.

2
REWIND

That night, Danny lay down in bed as he always did, flat on his back, with his cosmic remote clutched tightly to his chest.

He thought about his mother's threat to throw away everything in his room and wondered how his cosmic remote could possibly stop it happening.

He went through all the possibilities in his head: Pause, Rewind, Fast Forward, Record then Play, Rewind then Pause then Play again. Perhaps there were other combinations he hadn't tried yet. He had had the cosmic remote for six weeks and every day he felt that he had learned something new about how and where and when to use it.

He thought back to the day when he had been given the cosmic remote. It had been a birthday present from his Uncle Charlie. It had been his only birthday present except for a book about horses from his sister (which she had immediately borrowed and not given back) and a bottle of detergent from his parents.

The remote arrived in a small wooden crate marked "Fragile" with a total of twenty-seven different stamps on it. The stamps featured a range of weird-looking animals: camels with three humps, two-headed snakes, bright-pink horses, cows with wings and a creature with an elephant's trunk, a moose's antlers and huge back legs like a kangaroo. Danny looked at the postmark and the back of the box and the currency of the stamps, trying to work out which country the package had been sent from, but it was impossible to tell.

As soon as Mrs Danger saw the gift, she grunted, "What has my oafish brother bought him now?"

She didn't like
Uncle Charlie and
lived in constant
dread of him
coming to stay.
He'd turn up every
three or four months,

tanned and unshaven, wearing old clothes,
carrying a battered suitcase and smelling of
coffee and chocolate biscuits. He said he was a
salesman, but it wasn't clear what he bought or
sold, only that it involved visiting Britain for ten
days a year and travelling overseas for the other
three hundred-fifty-five. He'd merrily clump
through the Danger house, blundering into pot
plants and floor lamps, throwing himself into
armchairs with a thump and sending any
nearby cushions and doilies and footrests flying.

Mrs Danger would follow her brother
wherever he went, with a can of air freshener
tucked up her sleeve, releasing little squirts
every minute or so. When it was time to go,

Uncle Charlie would give Mrs Danger a thank-you present: usually something he'd picked up on his travels like a dress or bag or a vase. Mrs Danger would accept the gift with a weak smile and then burn it in the back garden after he'd gone.

Mrs Danger may have dreaded her brother's visits, but they were magical days for Danny. As soon as he saw his nephew, Uncle Charlie's face would light up. "Hey! Here he is, the man with the plan! What are we up to today, Danny boy?'

Uncle Charlie and Danny would spend the afternoon in the garden, pretending to be cavemen, building a shelter out of branches and leaves and garden chairs. They'd disappear into Danny's bedroom and imagine they were astronauts and make a rocket out of boxes and rugs and bedclothes. They'd take over the kitchen and tell Mrs Danger they were scientists and create a potion out of bleach and orange juice and flour and washing-up liquid.

The day that Danny remembered most clearly was when he and Uncle Charlie pretended to be detectives. Whenever he was feeling sad or angry, he would close his eyes and think back to that day. Uncle Charlie had brought lots of equipment with him: a magnifying glass, a notepad, a small tape recorder, a pair of binoculars. He taught Danny how to dust for fingerprints using a paintbrush and talcum powder. He took Danny's fingerprints using a pad of ink and then showed Danny how his prints showed up on glass and metal and plastic surfaces. He showed Danny how to make invisible ink out of lemon juice and how to copy a door key using soft putty. They followed Mrs Danger around the supermarket without her spotting them.

"How did you learn all this stuff, Uncle Charlie?" Danny whispered in the supermarket.

"I had an uncle – Uncle Percy – who taught me," Uncle Charlie whispered back, "and now I'm teaching you."

Occasionally, when Danny and Uncle Charlie were putting up a tent in the front garden or painting each other's faces in the living room, Danny's sister Mia would hover in the background, looking mildly curious and quietly intrigued. However, when Danny turned round and asked, "Do you want to join in?" Mia would look cold and distant and walk off haughtily.

"She's nice underneath it all," Uncle Charlie would always say. "She's just scared of showing it."

Once Eric had dropped round and shown Uncle Charlie how to rewire a remote control car so it went at twenty-five miles per hour.

"Hey, we could use someone like you!" Uncle Charlie had said.

"Who could?" asked Danny.

"Oh, just work, talking about work," Uncle Charlie had said quickly. "Come on, boys, let's test our new toy on the extension roof!"

When Uncle Charlie left, Danny was always in trouble because of all the mess and the noise and the state of the house and the state of the garden and what his poor mother had been put through and what his poor father had put up with. He'd be banished to his room for a week or made to hoover the hall and the stairs and the landing every morning for a fortnight. His weekends would be hell for about a month: he'd have to clean the glass on every single one of his mother's framed tea towels; he'd have to scrub and oil the tools in his father's shed; he'd have to polish the trophies in the living room that his sister had won for gymnastics.

But Danny didn't care. It was worth it for all the fun he had had when Uncle Charlie had come to stay. He'd think about Uncle Charlie's next visit and how all this cleaning and polishing didn't mean a thing because everything would soon be tipped over and mixed up and bashed about again.

So when his tenth birthday had come around and the present had arrived in the post, Danny knew it would be from Uncle Charlie and he knew it would be brilliant. His mother kept muttering to his father – they knew it would be trouble.

Danny picked up the box from the kitchen

table and took it upstairs to his room. There was no way he was going to open it in front of his parents. Mia tried not to look disappointed. His mother called after Danny, "If it makes a mess, we'll confiscate it."

As soon as he was inside his room, he threw the box on the ground and ripped it open. He clawed his way through the brown tape and the polystyrene swirls and the bubble wrap. He felt something hard and plastic with rubber buttons and a bump on the back. Finally he pulled out the cosmic remote and stared at it for a full minute before turning back to the package and seeing if there was anything else inside.

There was just a note from Uncle Charlie.

Dan the Man,

Thought this might be your kind of thing. Belongs to my work really, so look after it. Should come in handy next time your mum and dad give you grief. Keep it a secret though — unless there's an emergency.

See you in the spring, buster.

Uncle Charlie

Danny folded up the letter and put it in his pocket. It was strange to be given a birthday present that belonged to someone's work, but then this was Uncle Charlie so nothing was ever straightforward.

Danny turned the present over and over in his hand. The crystal on the back was pretty cool and it all fitted neatly into his hand and the buttons were satisfyingly chunky. But he couldn't help feeling a slight sense of disappointment. At the end of the day, it was just a remote control. Where was the thing it controlled?

Danny's disappointment vanished when he touched the Rewind button. The bubble wrap and polystyrene swirls leapt back into the box and the box resealed itself and started to hover above the floor and his bedroom door swung open. He let go of the Rewind button.

He pressed the Fast Forward button and the door swung shut and the box dropped to the floor and the bubble wrap leapt back out of the box and Danny began to hear footsteps drumming on the stairs.

He let go of Fast Forward and pressed Pause. The whole world stopped.

This was the best birthday present he had ever had.

He walked out of his room and on to the landing. He saw his mother and his father, halfway up the stairs, frozen in time, their faces twisted into strange expressions. His father's right foot was in mid-air, about to land on the stair above.

So many questions raced through Danny's mind. Why had the remote not flown back into the box when he pressed Rewind? If he was moving time backwards and forwards, why was he not affected? Why was he outside it all, watching events unfold?

If he could pause time, what happened to anything he touched or moved when time was paused? Did it fly back to its old position afterwards?

He laughed out loud. He was going to enjoy finding answers to these questions.

He looked down at the remote. For the first time he noticed the display flashing:

$$8{:}13\ldots\ 8{:}13\ldots\ 8{:}13\ldots$$

For the first time, he felt the crystal ticking round in his palm. There must be something magical hidden inside this box, Danny thought to himself.

He looked again at his parents, suspended halfway up the stairs. He had a thought. A thought that made him smile. Uncle Charlie was going to be proud of him.

He tripped down the stairs and undid his father's right shoelace. Then he squeezed past his parents and moved the table in the hall a few centimetres to the right. There was an assortment of vases and ornaments on this table; Danny moved them all a few centimetres to the left. He kicked up a corner of the rug in the hall, unhooked the latch that kept the cupboard under the stairs closed and moved everything in the cupboard forwards so that it was leaning precariously on the door. Then

Danny trotted back upstairs again, squeezed past his parents and hid behind the laundry basket on the landing. He pressed Play.

Life started up again. His father put down his right foot, and his lace was caught under his shoe; he lurched forwards and then toppled backwards. He fell on top of Danny's mother and they both bounced down the stairs. As they collapsed in the hall, Mrs Danger nudged the hall table that Danny had moved slightly to the right and all the vases and ornaments that Danny had moved slightly to the left toppled off the table and plummeted towards the floor. A china dog hit Mr Danger on the head and broke in two. Mrs Danger tried to catch a picture frame but fumbled and managed to snap it in half instead.

As they struggled to their feet, wailing and

roaring, Mrs Danger tripped over the rug in the hall that Danny had kicked over and flew forwards, her arms flailing, catching her knee on the door of the cupboard under the stairs. The cupboard swung open and the hoover and the ironing board and the mop and three buckets and several collapsible chairs dropped out.

The hoover broke open, releasing a billowing cloud of dust. The ironing board dropped open, burying one its legs in Mr Danger's stomach and another leg in Mrs Danger's neck. Mia rushed in from the kitchen and put her hand to her mouth, unable to believe her eyes.

Danny peered over the banister and called out innocently, "What's going on?"

He tried not to smile but it was hard. For the first time ever, there was mess everywhere and he could not be blamed for it. For the first time ever, looking at the plume of dust from the hoover and the broken ornaments on the floor and the plastic bucket wedged on his father's head, Danny felt at home in his parents' house.

***

Over the next few weeks, Danny experimented with his cosmic remote in all kinds of situations. At dinner times, he would wait till his family had finished their meals, and then press Rewind and watch everyone unchew their food, spit it gently on to their forks, and place it neatly back on their plates. At other times, when he had been banished to his room for two or three hours because he had sneezed without using a handkerchief or left a thumbprint on a glass of water, he would press Fast Forward until the time had passed and then come back downstairs, smiling broadly.

It took him a little longer to get the hang of the Record button. After a few days of pressing it and nothing happening, Danny was sitting on the front garden wall one morning when he accidentally squeezed the crystal on the back of the remote and heard something click. His thumb was hovering over the Record button at the time and he instinctively pushed it down. He was astonished when a beam of light shot out of the end of the remote and bathed the street with a yellow glow. He directed the beam at an old lady sitting in a car on the other side of the street. Nothing seemed to be happening to the car or the old lady, so after a few seconds he pressed Stop and the yellow beam disappeared and the crystal started to flash.

Danny forgot all about it until, later that day, he was sitting at his desk at school staring out the window. He pulled his cosmic remote out of his pocket and noticed that the crystal was still flashing. He tried pressing Record and then Stop and then Play. The crystal had stopped flashing but had anything else happened?

Then he heard one of his classmates say, "Sir, why's there an old lady in a car on top of that tree?"

Danny looked up and saw a shaft of light pouring out of the cosmic remote. The old lady in the car was hovering in the middle of the beam of light. Because of where the remote was pointing, it looked as if she was perched on top of the tree at the bottom of the school field. Danny pressed Stop as quickly as he could.

Danny's teacher, Mr Boswell, walked over to the window.

"What are you talking about, boy?" he snarled. "There's nothing there. One hundred lines: 'I must not tell lies in class'."

"Aw, sir," protested Danny's classmate.

"Another hundred lines: 'I must not answer back'," fumed Mr Boswell.

Danny looked down at his remote in amazement. There seemed to be no end to its powers.

As the weeks wore on, Danny began to think more deeply about what his remote was capable of. What if he pressed Rewind and kept pressing Rewind, would he slowly become seven and then six and then five, and gradually turn into a baby, still holding his cosmic remote? And what if he kept pressing Fast Forward, would he get older and older, until he was eighty or ninety or even a hundred, barely able to hold the remote in his twisted, trembling, old man's hands?

Danny might have tried this out – there were all kinds of experiments he wanted to run – but exactly a month after receiving the remote, something happened that made Danny more cautious about where and how he used his new toy.

It was a Sunday afternoon and Danny was walking down the stairs, quietly singing a song he had made up the day before:

When things go wrong,
don't scream and shout.
Press Rewind and wipe it out.
When life's a drag, don't lose your wits.
Fast Forward through the boring bits.
If you need to vanish – quick
Pressing Pause will do the trick.
For something wondrous and sublime,
Press Record to capture Time.
Hold down Stop and count to ten
Now you can watch it all again.

Danny headed towards the front door, thinking that he owed Eric a visit. He had half opened the door when he heard his mother's voice behind him.

"What's that for? And what's it doing on the floor?"

Danny turned round and froze. He had dropped his cosmic remote and it was lying in the middle of the hall. His mother was bending over to pick it up and his sister was standing in the kitchen doorway, looking bored.

"Nothing to do with me," said Mia. "Must be Danny's."

"It's m-mine, it's m-mine," stammered Danny, trying not to show how much he needed it back.

Mia suddenly looked more interested. "It *is* Danny's. Don't give it to him, Mum."

"I've no intention of giving it to him," said Mrs Danger.

"Please give it back," mumbled Danny desperately. "It's really important."

"If you drop it on the floor, then it must be rubbish," said Mrs Danger. "It's going in the bin."

Mia smiled, as if she had worked out why Danny was so afraid. "Press one of the buttons, Mum. Let's see what it does."

"No!" shouted Danny. He knew he had to do something drastic. He knew it didn't matter what he did, he could press Rewind and erase it all.

His mother's thumb hovered over the Play button; his sister looked over Mrs Danger's shoulder.

Danny ran over to one of the framed tea towels that was hanging in the hall. It said:

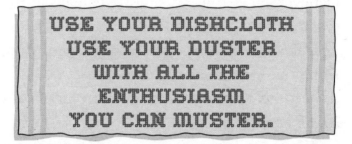

USE YOUR DISHCLOTH
USE YOUR DUSTER
WITH ALL THE
ENTHUSIASM
YOU CAN MUSTER.

He pulled it off the wall, threw it on to the floor and jumped up and down on top of it until the glass broke.

Mrs Danger was so shocked, she went as

stiff as a board and the remote slipped out of her hand. Danny dived forwards and tried to catch it before it hit the floor. Mia saw this and pushed her mother out of the way, determined to get to the remote before her brother. She clawed at the air like a cat, narrowly missing Danny's ear.

But Danny already had the remote in his hand and jammed his thumb on Rewind, letting out a huge sigh as all traces of the last two minutes were slowly wiped out, the tea towel was back on the wall, his mother was back in the living room and his sister was standing in the kitchen. He pressed Pause and positioned himself back on the stairs, holding his remote firmly in his right hand, certain he wouldn't drop it this time; that he wouldn't ever drop it again.

When he felt ready, he pressed Play and headed out to Eric's as he had planned, glancing at his mother and sister as they appeared in the hall. Danny couldn't help thinking they looked puzzled and slightly confused, as if they had a half-memory of what had nearly just happened.

***

Two days after that, something even more troubling happened to Danny.

It was late in the evening and Danny had spent the last couple of hours at his desk, finishing his homework and then drawing a comic strip about an alien for Eric.

He yawned and decided it was time for bed. He noticed that he hadn't drawn the curtains yet, so he got up from his chair and walked towards the window.

Then he stopped in his tracks.

Just outside his bedroom window he saw a pair of large yellow eyes, with thin black pupils. They stared into his room, not moving, not blinking.

Danny glanced down at the cosmic remote, sitting on the edge of his bed.

When he looked back up, the eyes had gone, and there was nothing outside his window, only darkness.

Danny rushed across to the window and

closed the curtains. Then he grabbed the remote, leapt into his bed, pulled the covers over his head and tried to calm down.

It was probably just an owl or a cat, he said to himself.

But the eyes were too big for an animal like that.

Perhaps they were lights from a plane or helicopter.

But they had seemed so close to his window.

He knew he could press Rewind, press Pause, and take a closer look at who or what those eyes belonged to. But that idea lasted about two seconds; he never wanted to look into those eyes again.

Another minute or so passed and Danny began to think more calmly about what he had seen. The eyes had appeared and disappeared in a flash. He wondered if he could have imagined the whole thing.

He had certainly been very tired. Maybe he had nodded off briefly and dreamed the last five minutes. He had also been anxious about his remote and other people finding out about what it could do. Maybe he'd imagined a burglar trying to break in and steal it.

By the time he went to sleep, he was pretty sure that nothing had happened and his mind had played tricks on him.

Besides, as long as he had his cosmic remote, nothing and nobody could hurt him.

3
FAST FORWARD

Back in the present day, Danny wondered what to do about his mother.

She was going to put everything in his room in a skip and he couldn't work out how to stop her.

The most obvious tactic was to let her cart everything off then press Pause and carry everything back into his room. But that would seem supernatural. He would draw attention to himself, his mother would be scared and suspicious, and before he knew it, she'd find his cosmic remote and smash it to pieces or, worse, work out how to use it and make his life more miserable than ever.

Danny looked out of his bedroom window; the skip had already arrived. It was standing in the street, empty except for a couple of paper cups that passers-by had idly tossed into it.

He looked down at the cosmic remote, willing it to come up with an answer.

He looked back out on to the street and saw his father opening one end of the skip to create a ramp. Mia appeared from the side gate pushing a wheelbarrow.

An idea popped into Danny's head. He wasn't sure if it would work or not. He held down the Pause button.

When everything froze, he skipped downstairs and out the front door. He couldn't resist giving his sister a gentle kick as he passed her. He crossed the street and headed for Eric's house. He climbed up the drainpipe, pressed Play and tapped on Eric's window.

"Hey, wotcha," said Eric, with a big smile. "Look at this."

Danny clambered into the room.

Eric picked up the robot they had started putting together the night before.

"I finished it this morning," said Eric. He flicked a switch on the robot's back and its eyes, mouth, arms, chest and legs lit up.

"Speech recognition," said Eric. "Walk forwards."

The robot trundled forwards.

"Turn left," said Eric.

The robot turned right.

"Turn left," demanded Eric.

The robot kept turning right.

"Bloomin' thing," mumbled Eric, and gave it an angry nudge.

"I think we put its legs on back to front," said Danny. "That's why it's confused."

"Did we?" said Eric, picking the robot up. "So we did."

He smiled at the robot. "Sorry, mate. We'll soon fix that."

Danny didn't have any time to lose.

"Listen, Eric," he said. "Can I ask you a favour?"

"Course," said Eric, holding a screwdriver in one hand and the robot in the other.

"You know your games room downstairs, with your table football in it and that," said Danny.

"Course," said Eric, sticking his tongue out with concentration as he loosened a screw.

"Can I store some of my things in there?" asked Danny. "It's just my mum's threatening to throw them out."

"Course," said Eric, pulling the robot's right leg off.

"And maybe keep it secret – you know, don't tell your parents," said Danny.

"Course not," said Eric. He put the robot on the ground. "That should do the trick."

He switched the robot on.

"Turn left," he said.

The robot turned right.

"Blast!" shouted Eric.

"We'll get used to it," said Danny. "When we want it to go left, we'll say go right."

Eric thought about this, then smiled. "Cool, yeah," he said. "Then nobody else will be able to work it."

"Exactly," said Danny. "So I'll move my stuff over, OK? I'll probably be pretty quick, you know, so my parents don't notice."

"No problem," said Eric. "Be as fast as you like."

Danny clambered out of Eric's window, checked that nobody could see him and pressed Pause.

He ran back across the street and into his house.

His parents and his sister were frozen on the landing, smiling broadly. They were clearly on their way to Danny's room. Danny pushed past them, giving his sister another gentle kick.

He spent the next two hours emptying his room. It required about fifty separate journeys. He carried as much as he could on each trip, piling it up in boxes and cases, heaving it down the stairs and across the street. He'd use his shoulder to push Eric's back door open, then haul everything across the kitchen into the games room, weaving past Eric's parents, who were standing rigidly in the hallway, holding gardening equipment.

By the time Danny had finished, he was utterly exhausted.

He stood in the middle of Eric's games room, sweat pouring off his brow, struggling to get his breath back. In the corner of the room, he saw his comics, toys, clothes, books, DVDs, posters, his lamp, his alarm clock and his radio.

When he'd got his strength back, he ran out of Eric's house and back across the street. He sprinted into his house and up the stairs. He pushed past his parents and sister (it was his father's turn for a gentle kick) and dived into his room, closing the door firmly behind him.

He sat on his bed and folded his arms. The room was completely bare except for his bed, his wardrobe and his desk. Not a single one of Danny's possessions remained.

Danny pulled out his remote, pressed Play and put it back into his pocket.

The door swung open and his parents and sister strode in.

"Hello," said Danny.

"What the—" stammered Danny's father.

"Crikey," said Mia, trying not to look hugely impressed.

"What have you done? What have you done?" blurted out his mother.

"I've tidied up," said Danny.

There were a few seconds of silence.

"The price of that skip's coming out of your pocket money," barked his father.

"How many times," sighed Danny. "You don't give me any pocket money."

"I don't know how you've done it," Danny's mother hissed, "but don't think for one moment you've got away with this. The minute I see anything – a comic, a poster – in this room, it's going in the bin."

Danny shrugged. "OK," he said.

The door was slammed shut.

His uncle's face popped into his head. He wanted to write him a letter and tell him all about this, but where would he send it? He didn't even know which country his uncle was in.

For the next few days, Danny managed to avoid his parents. He also managed to keep his room completely empty. He went everywhere with a small rucksack containing his school books, his favourite comics and a few bags of crisps. Whenever he left his room, he took his bag with him. When he was in his room, he kept his bag next to him in case his mother walked in.

After a week of this, Danny began to think hard about his life. How long would he have to keep his things at Eric's? Maybe using his cosmic remote and hiding all his possessions had only made matters worse. His parents disliked him more than ever.

But then, overnight, everything changed. Danny's parents quickly became the least of his worries, although they were, as always, the original cause of the problem.

Danny got into bed one night, pulled his duvet over his head and placed his remote under his pillow. Just as he was dropping off to sleep, he heard a quiet creaking noise. He opened his eyes and saw two dark shapes in his room. In terror, he yanked out his remote and pressed Pause.

He quickly calmed down when he realised that the two shapes were his parents. His mother was standing with one arm out, peering into his wardrobe. His father was frozen on all fours, peering under Danny's bed.

Danny lay back down again. He wondered how much his parents knew. He wasn't sure whether to slip out of the room, or stay and find out more. In the end, he held his remote tightly against his leg and pressed Play.

"Nothing under here," whispered his father.

"There must be something," his mother whispered back. "A secret compartment, or a trap door."

Danny relaxed. He closed his eyes and let his parents finish their search. When they left, he slipped his remote back under his pillow.

The next morning, Danny came downstairs early to get his breakfast. To his surprise, Mia was already sitting in the kitchen, staring at a letter. The letter was covered in green stains and patches of food.

When Danny murmured "Hi," she pushed it across the table to him.

"It's for you," she said.

Danny looked closer at the letter and saw his name, in Uncle Charlie's handwriting, underneath a squashed baked bean.

"It came yesterday," said Mia, "but Mum threw it in the bin. Said anything belonging to you was rubbish. I thought that was a bit – you know – a bit much. So I fished it out." Danny held the letter in two hands and stared at it. "It's from Uncle Charlie, isn't it?" his sister said.

Danny nodded and murmured, "I think so."

"You going to open it?" asked Mia.

"Mmm," said Danny.

At that moment, Eric appeared at the back door. Mia turned round and sighed. "What does that geekazoid want?"

"Hey, that's my friend you're talking about!" spat back Danny.

Eric opened the door and walked in. "Why are you talking to *her*, Danny?" asked Eric.

"Don't worry," said Mia. "I'm not staying in a room with you two in it. I've got my image to consider. Enjoy your letter, Danny. If Eric feels like breakfast, you could scrape the bits of egg off the back."

Danny had wanted to thank his sister for rescuing the letter, but now it was impossible. She was being her usual nasty self again.

As soon as Mia left the room, Danny tore open the letter. It read:

Sorry, Danny, forgot to say - don't use the remote between dusk and dawn. Just daytime. OK? Uncle Charlie.

Eric watched Danny reading and then said: "Your letter's a bit niffy, mate."

"Yeah," said Danny, absently. "Mum threw it in the bin." He was thinking about the night before when his parents had sneaked into his room. He had used the remote – but only briefly. Nothing bad had seemed to happen. He had pressed Pause and Play and they had both worked. Whatever Uncle Charlie was worried about, it didn't seem to have taken place.

Danny looked at Eric and wished he could tell him about the remote. But, although things were bad, it still didn't feel like an emergency. In any case, Eric wanted to talk about something else.

"Listen, Danny," he said. "I can't go to the park with you today."

"What?" said Danny. "How come?"

"I've got to go and see my Auntie Gladys," said Eric. "It's so annoying. She gives me these horrible sloppy kisses. And squeezes my cheeks so hard my whole face goes numb."

"Blimey," said Danny.

"So I've got five minutes, then I've got to go," said Eric.

"Oh," said Danny. "See you tomorrow, though?"

"Definitely," replied Eric. "We're back tonight."

The two boys talked about Eric's robot for a couple of minutes, then Eric left.

A few minutes after that, Danny went upstairs and got his rucksack from his room. He decided to go to the park on his own. He didn't want to stay in the house, that was for sure.

It was about nine o'clock when he arrived at the gates. The park was a large square patch of grass with trees around the edge, a slide and some swings in one corner and a duck pond in the middle. Danny noticed a few children flying kites at the far end. There were also a couple of old ladies sitting on one of the benches by the gate.

Danny walked towards the swings. He took the path next to the duck pond and remembered being five or six and asking his mother if he could feed the ducks. She had said no because he would get crumbs everywhere and besides ducks were scruffy and uncouth.

He was about halfway round the duck pond when he began to feel very uncomfortable. He wondered if he needed to eat something or if he had eaten something that hadn't agreed with him. He shivered and felt the colour drain out of his face. He kept walking, hoping that this would help him to shake off his strange mood.

But as he reached the edge of the duck pond, he realised that he was feeling worse not better. It was as if the air around him had grown colder. He also felt as if he was being watched or followed though he couldn't see anyone on the path behind him or in the bushes around him.

Then something in the duck pond caught his eye. He turned round and saw a small black dot right in the centre of the water. As he stood there, trying to work out what it was, it grew larger. The ducks all seemed to be avoiding it; they began to paddle towards the bank. The shape was the size of a football now, rising slowly towards the surface of the pond. The water began to hiss slightly, and Danny could smell something tangy and metallic. The shape was rising more quickly now, growing larger and darker, until its outline grew more clear and something bright and black broke the surface of the pond.

Danny glanced around to see if any other people were nearby. He needed someone else to confirm that this was actually happening. But nobody was walking or even looking this way – he was on his own.

He forced himself to look back at the pond. Floating on the surface was the biggest, blackest fish he had ever seen, at least as big as he was. It had large red eyes that stared balefully ahead and sharp yellow spikes that ran along its back. As Danny gazed in disbelief, he also noticed a row of metal rivets above its jaw and steel slats behind its eyes that acted like gills. It seemed to be half-fish and half-machine. This didn't make Danny feel any less afraid – in fact, he now felt as if he was in genuine danger.

He was about to run away, then he nearly called for help, then he thought he should press Pause on his cosmic remote first and work out a plan—

The next moment, Danny no longer had any choice.

The fish's eyes began to rotate, sending out shards of multicoloured light. Danny tried to look away, but the colours were so stunning. He was no longer able to move or speak: he just stood rooted to the ground, hypnotised.

A cloud of steam poured out of the fish's gills and its jaws began to move apart, revealing a gigantic black mouth, half the length of its body. When the fish's jaws were fully open, it was almost as if the creature was inside out, with two rows of metal ribs clearly visible at the back of its throat.

The next few moments were as vivid and as unreal as a dream. Danny sensed his hand moving towards his pocket. He felt very strongly that he should throw his cosmic remote into the fish's mouth. He pulled the remote out of his pocket and lifted his arm up. He knew he needed to concentrate: he had to hit the centre of the fish's mouth so that it could swallow the remote whole and swim away with it safely.

Danny took aim. He swung his arm back once, twice, three times.

He couldn't understand why he didn't want to let go of his cosmic remote.

The fish released another cloud of smoke from its iron gills.

Danny took aim for a second time and

swung his arm back. He was about to release the remote and send it spiralling through the air when he felt his fist close tightly around the case and the crystal glow warmly in his palm.

He seemed to wake up, jerking his head back and gasping loudly for air.

He looked at the fish and the pond and the remote in his hand and pressed Pause.

He seemed only half aware of what had just happened. He quickly pressed Rewind, which closed the fish's mouth, sent it back into the water and returned the ducks to the middle of the pond. Then he pressed Pause again.

He sat down on the grass and took four or five deep breaths. He still felt afraid. He took another five deep breaths.

He couldn't believe he had nearly thrown his cosmic remote away. He looked down at the remote and felt like apologising to it.

He also couldn't believe a gigantic metal fish had just appeared in his local park. This meant that someone had built it and someone had put it in the pond. But who?

Danny slowly retraced his steps through the park. He didn't know which way to go. Part of him wanted to run straight home and sit in his empty room with the door shut tight. Another part of him wanted to go back to the pond and take on the fish, throwing rocks at its head till it sank.

But mostly he needed time and space to gather his thoughts. He cast his mind back to where he had been standing five minutes previously. He positioned himself in roughly the right place – just in front of the park entrance – and pressed Play. Birds started to sing again; trees swayed in the breeze. He saw an empty bench a few metres away. He sat down and looked down at his shoes, holding the remote to his chest.

Danny whispered to himself: "You're OK. You're OK." He began to feel his confidence returning.

He watched a jogger pass in front of him. A minute later, a young woman strolled past with a baby strapped to her front. Danny glimpsed the duck pond in the distance and shuddered. An awful thought occurred to him. Maybe the fish could crawl out of the pond and across the grass. Maybe he'd lose his remote this time.

But another glance at the duck pond was enough to calm his nerves. He was safe where he was. Besides, there were more people in this part of the park; they'd notice if he was attacked again, especially by a giant robot fish.

Danny let another couple of minutes pass by. He wondered whether life would ever get back to normal or whether he'd always feel like something strange was about to happen.

He looked up and saw, about twenty metres in front of him, a small dog with its nose to the ground, sniffing frantically, following a scent. It headed in Danny's direction, snuffling more loudly, gathering speed as the scent it had picked up grew stronger. The dog was coming straight at Danny now, its nose glued even more tightly to the ground, its jowls trembling as its snorts grew more frantic.

It reached Danny's bench and started to

sniff behind it and beside it and underneath it, wedging its nose in between the wooden slats, coating the paintwork with drool. Then it stopped in front of the bench and stared at the remote in Danny's hand. It barked once and waited. When Danny didn't react, it barked again.

Now that dog had stopped moving, Danny was able to look at it more closely. Its fur was thick and wiry; its legs were short and sturdy; its eyes were big and friendly. It was like a cross between a spaniel and a terrier. Just as Danny was about to stroke it and pat its head, he noticed a tangle of wires hanging out of one of its ears. He looked at its face and saw that its tongue was a strip of red rubber, its nose was a golf ball and its whiskers were pipe cleaners.

Danny leapt up as if the bench was on fire. He looked down at the dog and looked around to see who was controlling it. Just as he was about to run away, the dog's tail began to wag. It moved back and forth, back and forth, as if it were beating out the rhythm of a song. Danny tried to pull his eyes away, but found himself captivated by the movement of the dog's tail. The tail continued to wag, and Danny kept staring at it, until he felt all his muscles relaxing and all the tension leaving his body. The tail carried on swinging from side to side, as Danny smiled at the dog, and smiled at the park, and smiled up at the sky.

The dog barked, Danny looked down at his cosmic remote and decided to throw it through the air like a stick. The dog would fetch it and bring it back to him. He pulled his arm back, determined to throw the remote as hard and as far as he could.

"You ready, boy?" he said in a dreamy voice.

The dog yapped cheerfully.

"You going to fetch it?" murmured Danny.

The dog woofed again.

Danny looked into the distance and wondered what to aim for: the flowerbed by the bandstand or the bushes next to the swings? He thought the dog would have more fun if it had to hunt for the remote.

He prepared for his throw, arching his back and straining the muscles in his arm.

"Fetch!" he shouted, just as he was about to relax his grip.

But Danny couldn't let go of the remote. He just couldn't let go.

Instead, a snatch of time flashed inside his head, as if he had pressed Fast Forward. He saw the dog bounding across the park, he saw it grab the remote, he saw the dog run out of the park, he saw it tearing through fields and forests and he saw it burying the remote on a gloomy, windswept heath, where nobody had ventured for years.

A split second later, the dog's tail fell off with a clunk.

Danny came to his senses. The dog seemed to half realise what had happened. It flung itself through the air and snatched the remote out of Danny's hand. Danny lurched forwards and caught hold of one of the dog's back legs. The leg came off in Danny's hand and the dog froze in mid-leap and dropped with a thump to the ground. Smoke poured slowly out of its ears and mouth. Danny looked down and saw a dozen batteries packed into the dog's hollow leg. He pulled the remote out of the dog's rigid jaws and pressed Pause.

The park was calm and still again.

Danny now knew that everything had changed. The fish could have been a freak event but the fish and the dog together left Danny in no doubt; somebody knew about his cosmic remote and somebody was determined to get it.

He suddenly remembered how he used the

remote in the middle of the night. He wondered if that had triggered something. Or had his sister guessed what his secret was? Had she told someone else? In a way, it didn't matter; all that mattered was that everything was different now.

There would probably be more robot creatures sent to attack him. They would probably get fiercer and more frightening as time went on.

Unless, of course, Danny handed over the remote.

Danny looked down at the remains of the remote-controlled dog. He might have to fight something like that every day for the rest of his life.

Then he looked at his cosmic remote. He knew he'd never give it to anyone else. Never.

Danny walked through the town slowly. The world was still paused: cars were motionless in the middle of roads; people stood like statues on pavements and driveways.

He wouldn't know where to go until he had worked out what to do next.

He was in no hurry to press Play. He wondered when he would feel ready to press Play.

As he turned into a side street, he thought he saw a pair of bright yellow eyes, staring at him from deep inside a hedgerow. They were the same yellow eyes that had appeared in his bedroom window a few weeks before. But when he looked at the hedge again, they were gone.

For the first time ever, he didn't feel safe, even when he had pressed Pause. Even when he had stopped the world, and he was the only person moving, he felt as if there were another pair of footsteps echoing behind his.

4
RECORD

There was a footpath that ran behind Danny's house, lined with tall trees. Danny chose the tallest tree and climbed it as quickly as he could, scrambling from branch to branch until he had reached the very top. In front of him he could see his house, his street, the park and the town beyond. Behind him, he saw rows of gardens and the back of his school. If anyone started looking for him, he would see them coming from miles away. He was ready to press Play.

When everything sprang back to life, Danny tensed up, glancing around frantically for anything that could be a threat.

He scanned every bird in the sky, every car on the street and every face in every window. The tree gave an ominous creak and for a split second Danny wondered if it too was a robot: it would lift up its roots and stamp off down the street, carrying Danny away to its master.

A few minutes passed. A car drove by in the next street. The lady next door appeared in her garden with a basket full of washing for the line. Nothing seemed unusual or out of place.

Another minute passed. Danny felt calmer. He could stay in the tree until he had found somewhere safer to hide out.

His heart jumped when he saw a shape appear at the end of the footpath. He relaxed when he realised it was his sister. He'd forgotten that she came this way home after her Saturday morning diving lesson: right off the high street, left down the footpath, through the back garden to open the kitchen door.

He closed his eyes, hoping that his sister wouldn't spot him.

When he opened them again, his sister was

standing at the bottom of the tree, looking straight up at him.

"You're not allowed to climb trees," said Mia. "I'm telling Mum." She turned to walk away.

"N-no, wait, Mia," called out Danny, and whipped his remote out of his pocket, then pressed Pause.

This wasn't good. He had to stop Mia from reaching the house, but how could he stop her without leaving the safety of the tree? He wasn't sure if he'd be able to stop her even if he *could* leave the tree. Short of telling her about the remote, he couldn't think of anything else that would make her listen to him.

At that moment, something Uncle Charlie had said popped into Danny's head: "She's nice underneath it all. She's just scared of showing it." He also remembered the way she had fished Uncle Charlie's letter out of the bin. Danny realised that it was time to tell his sister about the remote.

Two seconds later, an idea dropped into his

head, fully formed.

He pressed Rewind until Mia was a few minutes away from the end of the footpath. Then he pressed Pause again.

He was going to use the remote's multiple recording capability, something he had only tried once or twice before. This was when you recorded several stretches of time one after the other, then released them all at the same time by pressing Play. Not just one, but three or four or five images would shoot out of the end of the remote.

He started to climb down the tree. Even though he had paused everything, he still looked round every few seconds for anything that might pounce or swoop.

When he reached the ground, he walked across to the gate that joined the footpath to his back garden, and slipped inside.

He walked up the garden path towards the house and stopped in front of the back door. Then he turned his remote round, pointed it at himself, and pressed Record. He made sure he was standing inside the beam of yellow light.

He stood still for a few seconds and then shook his head and said, "I wouldn't go this way if I were you, Mia."

He stood still for another ten seconds and then pressed Stop.

He slipped out of the gate and on to the footpath. He climbed back up the tree with the remote between his teeth. When he reached the top, he breathed a sigh of relief, feeling considerably safer now he could see everything again.

He pressed Play on his remote. A few minutes passed, and his sister appeared at the end of the footpath. He pointed the remote straight at her and pressed Record. He kept the beam of light trained on her as she walked towards the tree. When she spotted him, he pressed Stop.

"You're not allowed to climb trees," said Mia.

Danny pushed the crystal in his remote till he heard it click.

"I'm telling Mum," said Mia.

Danny pressed Play. This released the two stretches of time: Mia walking down the path and Danny standing by the back door.

"Mia, look!" shouted Danny. "Behind you!"

Mia gave Danny a bored look and turned round slowly. She froze with fear when she saw another Mia walking calmly down the footpath.

"What the—? That's not possible..."

She ran towards the gate that led into the back garden. The second Mia was still heading straight for her.

She opened the gate, dived into the back garden and slammed the gate shut. The recording of Danny standing by the back door was still playing.

Mia looked up in disbelief. Danny was blocking her path, shaking his head. "I wouldn't go this way if I were you, Mia."

"How – how did you get down here so fast?" stammered Mia.

Then she turned round and saw Danny, still sitting in the tree.

"Two – two places at once..." she whispered.

She looked at Danny in the garden and Danny in the tree and seemed to make a sudden decision. She ran back towards the gate and flung it open. She looked round for the other Mia, but there was no sign of her. So she sprinted towards the tree next to Danny's and climbed it as quickly as she could.

This was exactly what Danny had hoped she would do.

When Mia reached the top of the tree, she spent a few seconds staring at nothing, getting her breath back.

"Mia," said Danny.

"Mia," he said, more loudly.

Mia looked across at Danny. Their trees were

about four metres apart.

"Mia," said Danny. "I know I've freaked you out, but listen to me."

"Uh-huh," said Mia, blankly.

"What just happened was because of this gadget I've got," said Danny. "It's called a cosmic remote."

"Uh-huh," said Mia again.

Danny began to wonder if his plan had been a mistake. His sister seemed to be in deep shock and incapable of understanding anything. Perhaps she was the wrong person to tell; perhaps he should rewind the last ten minutes. But he kept on.

"Mia, listen, this remote – it's like a TV or DVD remote, but I can actually use it to move time around. That's how I could appear in two places at once. And make you appear in two places at once," said Danny.

"Two places at once, yeah," murmured Mia.

"I know it seems hard to believe, but honestly, it really can do anything. Move time forwards and backwards. Stop time too. It still blows my mind – and I've had it for two months now," Danny went on.

"Two months now," said Mia wonderingly.

"But listen, Mia. Someone's found out about it. And they're sending robot animals after me. And I don't know how long I can keep fighting them off. That's why I'm up this tree."

The word "tree" seemed to snap Mia out of her trance.

"What am I doing in a tree?" she said, looking at Danny and then down at the branch she was sitting on.

"It's OK, Mia," said Danny. "You climbed up the tree about two minutes ago. Because I used my cosmic remote."

"You did what?" said Mia, smiling vaguely. "I must say, that sounds highly unlikely."

"Now, Mia, I want you to stay calm. But I'm going to use the Pause button on my remote to disappear from this branch and reappear on that branch over there."

He pointed at a thick leafy bough on the tree that Mia was in.

"Do what you like," sniffed Mia. "I'm getting down from this tree before Mum sees me."

Danny pressed Pause, crawled across the tree, settled himself on the bough next to Mia's and pressed Play.

"Wha–what?" Mia stammered, her eyes wide and her mouth open. She seemed to remember what had just happened on the ground with two Dannys and two Mias and nothing making sense.

"Tell me the bit about the remote again," she said, with a frown.

So Danny told her again about the remote and what it could do.

"So that's how you managed to empty your room so quickly yesterday," said Mia.

Danny nodded. "With the Pause button."

"And that's why there's been so many accidents at home: Mum falling over, Dad dropping things..." said Mia.

Danny nodded. "That would mostly have been me."

"Hmmph," said Mia, and seemed to be thinking to herself.

"And you just have one of those remote things?" she said.

Danny nodded.

"Not two?" she said.

Danny shook his head. "I think this is the only one in existence," he added.

The wind blew gently through the trees and Danny and Mia were rocked back and forth.

Danny began to tell Mia about what had happened in the park, describing the fish and the dog in vivid detail.

When he had finished, Mia took a deep breath and said, "So now you need my help."

Danny shrugged and said, "Mmm."

"To watch your back. To look out for you," said Mia.

"Mmm," said Danny again.

"So what if I don't help? You'll zap me with your remote?" said Mia.

"No, no," protested Danny. "I mean, not unless you tell Mum about it or something."

Mia nodded slowly. "I'll think about it," she said and started to climb down the tree.

Halfway down she flinched and said, "Did you just do something?"

"No, no, I swear," said Danny, holding the remote up.

Mia kept climbing down, fixing Danny with a stern glare.

Danny watched his sister walk across the garden and go into the house. A few seconds later she appeared in her bedroom window, still looking at Danny suspiciously.

He wondered if telling his sister had made him feel better or worse. He certainly didn't feel any safer.

He sat in the tree for ages, watching the sun move across the sky.

At about six o'clock, he picked up a strong smell of food. He looked down and spotted a plate of sausage and mash sitting at the bottom of the tree.

Glancing up, he saw his sister walking back towards the house. He held up his hand to say thanks but Mia had already shut the kitchen door.

As he sat at the top of the tree eating his dinner, Danny realised that the light would not last much longer. If he didn't think of a plan of action soon, he'd be spending the whole night outside, trying to stay warm and stay awake.

The sun went behind a cloud and Danny shivered. At that moment, his remote began to ring like a phone. Danny balanced his empty plate on a branch and pulled it out of his pocket.

The ringing tone seemed to be coming from the crystal on the back of the remote. He wasn't sure what it meant or how to stop it.

He tried pressing Play and the time display began to expand, getting deeper and wider until it was the size of a small screen.

Then Uncle Charlie's face appeared on it.

"Hello Danny," he said. "Long time no see. How you been?"

"Uncle Charlie!" exclaimed Danny. "What … how… I mean, how are you talking through the remote...?"

"The remote's got a special code number. As long as you know it, you can make a video call. Anyway, listen, I only have about 30p of credit left, so I have to be quick. Something's happened, Danny. There's this person that wants the remote and I think they've found out where it is. I'm not sure how."

"I – I – think it was me. I used it at night," said Danny.

"Oh, right. You didn't get my letter, eh?"

"Yeah, but Mum threw it away."

"My sister! I should have known! Well, it's my fault too. I should have told you right at the start. I should have told you everything."

"Tell me now," said Danny.

"I'm down to 18p, but I'll do my best. I work for an organisation called EUREKA!

We look after people's gadgets. You see, there are some pretty incredible gadgets out there – they can control people's thoughts, beam people on to the surface of the moon. One of the gadgets we look after is the cosmic remote."

"So – OK – so – how come you're allowed to give it to me?"

"We're allowed to lend the gadgets to people who really need them. People in trouble. People who will look after them and use them only for good. That means you. But I've put you in grave danger. I thought the Night Scientist—"

"The Night what?"

"The Night Scientist. He's a criminal genius, and he's tried to steal our gadgets in the past. He's tall with a white coat. He has a bald head and these piercing yellow eyes."

"Yellow eyes? Uncle Charlie, I think I've seen him!"

"What do you mean?"

"Well, I saw something with yellow eyes—"

"Listen Danny, I'm coming now. Hide till I get there. Be everywhere and nowhere. You understand? Use the remote."

Then his uncle's face disappeared from the screen. He had dropped his phone, and Danny could only see feet and table legs.

"Charles Baker, we meet at last," came a thin, cackling voice.

"How did you find me?" said Uncle Charlie's voice.

"I've known your hiding place for days," said the cackling voice, "and now I know where the remote is too. For heaven's sake, Charles, you should have warned them not to use it at night. You know that's when I 'take the air'. Now, before I go and claim my prize, I wish to dispose of you."

"Interesting idea. Let me know how it pans out," said Uncle Charlie.

"Uncle Charlie!" called out Danny. "Uncle Charlie!"

Then there was a crackling noise and the screen went black. It gradually whirred and shrank until it just displayed the time again.

Danny jabbed at the Play button, trying to

get Uncle Charlie's voice back, but nothing happened.

Something bad was happening to Uncle Charlie, and there was nothing he could do.

Danny tried not to cry, but it was difficult.

They would catch Danny too, and Uncle Charlie would not be able to rescue him.

Danny looked at the remote and felt like breaking it into pieces. If he'd never seen it, he'd still have Uncle Charlie. He wondered if breaking it would stop the evil man and save his uncle.

He was about to hurl it out of the tree when he saw his sister standing on the grass in the middle of the back garden.

"I've decided I'll help you," she called out. "What do you need me to do?"

This brought Danny back from the edge. Uncle Charlie would be OK – he had to believe that. Uncle Charlie would come and find him – he had to believe that, too.

Uncle Charlie's advice, "Be everywhere and nowhere" rushed into his head and suddenly

Danny knew what he had to do.

He climbed down the tree and walked towards Mia.

"Before we get started," said Mia, "I thought we should agree a few basic rules. First, I'd rather you didn't make two of me again. Second, I'm allowed to borrow the remote once a week – maybe Sunday afternoons? – and—"

"Mia, we haven't got time for this," interrupted Danny. "Uncle Charlie's in trouble and something called a Night Scientist is after me."

"A what is after you?" said Mia. "It was a giant fish a few hours ago."

"Well, both of them must be after me," said Danny. "Now, Uncle Charlie gave me a message and I think I know what he meant. I've got to look like I'm everywhere. I'll have to record myself – like I did earlier today."

"Hang on," said Mia. "How did Uncle Charlie give you a message? You've been up that tree all afternoon."

Danny ignored Mia's question. "So I need

you to distract Mum while I set up some decoys."

"Distract Mum?" replied Mia, pulling a face. "I don't know if I'd be very good at that."

"Oh go on, Mia," Danny pleaded. "You said you'd help."

Mia sighed. "Yes. I suppose I did."

Danny smiled at Mia and she gave a half-smile back. A thought seemed to strike her and she turned on her heel and strode back into the house.

Danny turned the remote round and began to record himself. He captured a version of himself standing by the shed and another version sitting on the back door step. He recorded himself hiding in the bushes, leaning on the back gate and perching on the patio wall.

Every now and again he would look around to see

if there were any suspicious animals or objects in sight. He could have pressed Pause before he made his recordings. But he wanted the decoy Dannys to look as real as possible, with movement around them, not everything frozen in mid-air.

He opened the back door and stepped warily inside the kitchen. There was no sign of his mother.

Then he heard voices in the bathroom above him.

"No, Mum, you missed a bit. There's still a really faint ring around the bath," he heard his sister say.

"You're right, Mia," said his mother. "Well spotted. I'd better clean the whole bathroom again. Just to be on the safe side."

Danny smiled. "Good thinking, Mia," he said to himself.

Danny recorded himself standing in the kitchen and in the hall. He recorded three versions of himself in the lounge and four in the dining room. He recorded himself standing on every step of the staircase, including three versions of himself on the top stair. He recorded himself in his sister's room, his parents' room and in the spare room. He walked into his bedroom and, for the first time, was glad that it was completely empty. It gave him more space to record himself by the window, by the wardrobe, in the wardrobe, on the bed, under the bed, behind the door, leaning on the window ledge and standing squarely in the middle of the room.

When he'd finished, he noticed that it was dark outside. He slipped out of his room and on to the landing. At the same time, his sister slipped out of the bathroom, closing the door gently behind her.

"I told Mum there was mould on the shower curtain," whispered Mia. "She'll be in there for another hour."

"Great!" replied Danny.

"What now?" Mia asked.

Danny looked down at the time on his cosmic remote: **7:20:34**.

"Dad will be home in ten minutes," said Danny. "I'd better stay in my room for the rest of the evening. After everyone's gone to bed, I'll move downstairs. I need to keep watch on the front door – and the back door – and anywhere else where someone might try to get in."

"So what are you going to do?" Mia asked. "Stand in the middle of the kitchen all night? That's not exactly blending into the background, is it?"

"I'm going to crawl inside the washing machine," said Danny.

"You're going to what?" spluttered Mia.

"It's the best place! It's right in the middle of the kitchen and I can see everything through the glass," said Danny.

"But Mum has the washing machine going all night. It never stops," protested Mia.

"That's why I'd like *you* to pour *soup* into the dispenser," said Danny. "That should put it out of action for a while."

"You're not serious?" said Mia. "You want me to break the washing machine. Mum's washing machine. The only thing in the world she truly loves."

Danny nodded.

"Unless you want me to do it," he said.

A smile spread slowly across Mia's face. "No. I think I can take care of it."

She smiled again and walked towards the stairs. On the top stair she turned round.

"Any particular *kind* of soup?" she asked.

Danny rubbed his chin. "I think I saw a tin of fish stew in the cupboard."

Mia nodded. "I'll find it," she said, and went downstairs.

Danny went back inside his room and sat on the bed. Every now and again he heard his mother growling and squeaking as she scrubbed away in the bathroom. Five minutes later, his sister opened his bedroom door.

"All done," she said.

"Thanks, Mia," said Danny. "That's great."

"Is there anything else?" she asked.

"No, no," said Danny. "I just have to wait now. Watch and wait."

"Well, I suppose if there's anything else," said Mia, "you know where I am."

Danny nodded.

"You owe me one, right?" she said.

Danny nodded again.

"See you around," she said, and closed the door.

5
STANDBY

At about eight in the evening, Danny heard raised voices downstairs. He guessed that his mother had discovered her washing machine wasn't working. Sure enough, he heard his father protesting: "I didn't touch it, I didn't go near it, I don't even know how it works."

An hour after that, he heard his parents traipsing upstairs. He turned his bedroom light off so they wouldn't guess he was inside. He heard Mia trudging upstairs too and then people taking turns in the bathroom. Half an hour after that, everything was silent.

Danny swung his legs off the bed and felt his

way across the room in the darkness. He found the handle of his bedroom door and turned it. By the time he stepped on to the landing his eyes were more accustomed to the darkness and he could make out doors and windows and the edges of furniture.

He slid into the bathroom, picked up two towels from the radiator and padded downstairs. He crept into the kitchen and knelt down in front of the washing machine. His mother had bought one of the biggest models on the market so there was enough space in the drum for two Dannys and possibly Mia too. Danny climbed inside and wrapped his face and body in the towels from the bathroom so that it looked as if the washing machine was full of regular laundry. Everything was in place for the night ahead.

Danny peered through the glass of the washing-machine door. By staring straight ahead, he could see everything in the kitchen and half of the dining room. By looking to the left, he could see the back door and the patio windows. By looking to the right, he could see the hallway, the front door and part of the living room.

He spent twenty minutes scanning the door knobs and window handles for movement. Everything was silent and still. He felt his eyelids drooping. The remote slipped out of his hand and hit the washing-machine drum with a thunk, and he sprang awake.

When he realised what had happened, he tucked the remote into his pocket, pressed his nose against the glass door and fell asleep again.

He dreamed he was a dog and that he was scratching a flea on his neck with his back leg. Slowly he realised he could actually hear scratching. His eyes flicked open.

The noise was coming from behind the kitchen skirting board. It got louder and more frantic. Finally a mouse appeared from a crack in the wall next to the back door. It scampered across the kitchen floor, right in front of the washing-machine door. That's when Danny noticed that it was a mouse with blue crystal eyes, thin iron legs and a crooked metal aerial where its tail would normally be. Danny looked up and saw another mouse scuttling through the living-room door. A third then skittered down the dining-room wall like a lizard. All three mice lined up on the front door mat.

The letter box flipped open and Danny saw a pair of cruel yellow eyes staring into the house. The letter box flipped shut.

The mice scrambled up the front door, one dived inside the key hole, one scuttled towards the chain and one headed for the latch. Their tails twitched as they gnawed and burrowed. There was a click and the door swung open. There, standing on the doorstep, was a man in a long white coat.

His head was bald and his skin was so white that in places you could see networks of arteries and veins trembling below the surface. His yellow eyes scanned the hallway. Then he spoke.

"Well done, Hubert. Good work, Arthur. Many thanks, Montgomery."

The three mice were standing in a line next to him.

Danny shuddered. Even through the glass of the washing-machine door, he recognised the voice. It was the same voice he had heard when Uncle Charlie phoned him on the remote. It was the same voice that had threatened to kill Uncle Charlie.

Did that mean Uncle Charlie was – definitely – not going to come – ever?

Danny felt suddenly terrified. He clung on to the remote, his thumb hovering over the Play button.

"I can't believe the owner of the cosmic remote lives in such a poky little shack," the bald man drawled. "I was expecting something on a grander scale."

He clicked his fingers and the mice scrambled up his body and disappeared into three different pockets of his coat.

He stepped into the house.

"Now, let's see if we're getting warm," he said. He had a small square box in his hand, which he flipped open. It beeped once, and then again, and then again. He flipped it closed.

"Now, the cosmic remote was used yesterday morning at 5:05. That gave me its unique code number," he said with a smile. "My portable object locator tells me that a remote with that code number is a mere ten metres from where I'm standing. Now, where-oh-where could it be?"

He strode through all the downstairs rooms, flinging cushions off the sofa, up-ending chairs and yanking open cupboard doors. He walked straight past the washing machine.

Danny lost sight of him when he went upstairs.

Danny was tempted to climb out of the washing machine now and either hide somewhere else or run away. But he was too scared to make a decision.

Time seemed to slow down or even stop, as if he had pressed Pause on his remote. Was the bald man still in the house?

Danny flinched. The bald man was back in the kitchen, looking at the box in his hand.

"The signal's strongest in here," said the man.

OK, Danny thought, *now is the moment*. He pressed Play on his remote and watched a forest of Dannys springing up, scattered across the kitchen and dining room, sprinkled through the living room and hallway.

He could not see them but he knew that all the Dannys on the staircase and in the bedrooms upstairs would also have been released from the remote.

The bald man spun round and lunged at the nearest Danny.

"Gotcha," he said, but his hand grabbed nothing but air.

He lurched at the Danny by the back door.

Once more, his hand passed clean through the recorded Danny and out the other side.

"Curses," spat the bald man.

Danny could not help but smile as he watched the bald man fumbling around in the gloom.

"One of them must be real," growled the man. "One of them must be holding the remote."

The bald man ran at every Danny he could see, swiping and grasping and lashing out.

Then he seemed to see all the Dannys standing on the stairs.

"OK, enough of this," he snarled. "I'm going to wait till they all vanish. The last one standing will be the boy I want."

Danny hadn't thought of this. He wondered if he should press Pause and then Rewind and start the whole evening again. But what if his uncle was on his way after all? And hadn't his uncle wanted him to hide?

A few seconds passed. Danny watched the versions of himself in the kitchen vanish. The three Dannys in the living room burst like bubbles, then the Dannys in the hallway fizzled out.

The bald man smiled and put his foot on the bottom stair. He sang out:

"Put it in a letter, write it in a note.

It's time to say goodbye
to your cosmic remote."

He put his foot on the next stair.

"Everything is fabulous, everything is fine.

In less than thirty seconds,
the remote will be mine."

The bald man trotted up the stairs, as the Dannys flickered and went out in front of him.

Danny couldn't help himself. He climbed out of the washing machine and dashed into the hall.

Surely the bald man's singing had woken his parents up? He couldn't decide whether he wanted this to happen or not. But he couldn't hear any noise coming from upstairs, except for the bald man humming and gently opening doors.

It was time to run. Every muscle and nerve in his body told him it was time to run. But his legs wouldn't move.

The bald man was coming back downstairs and Danny was standing in the middle of the hall. He wanted to press something on his remote but he couldn't decide which button or when or what he wanted to happen when he pressed it.

The bald man stepped off the bottom stair and swivelled on his heel.

"Now, let me guess," he drawled. "Charles Baker's son – or nephew – or younger brother?"

Danny didn't reply.

"Oh well, it's of no importance," sniffed the bald man. "Just hand me the cosmic remote and I'll leave you and your family in peace."

Danny looked at the man's yellow eyes and papery skin and shuddered in horror.

"Where's my Uncle Charlie?" Danny whispered.

"Give me the remote and I'll tell you," said the bald man.

"No. Tell me now," breathed Danny.

"Give me the remote or you'll be meeting him sooner than you think," said the bald man.

He stared at the remote in Danny's hand. A smile tugged at the corner of his mouth and one of his legs began to twitch with excitement.

Danny took one step backwards. The bald man took two steps forwards. Danny took two steps backwards. The bald man took three steps forwards. Danny's mind was suddenly clear. He was going to press Pause and run away when he heard a creak on the landing. He looked up and saw his sister making her way nervously down the stairs.

"Danny," she murmured. "What's going on? Is there someone there with you?"

"Run away, Mia!" Danny whispered urgently. "Get out of here!"

"Has that man come for you?" asked Mia.

"The Mighty Scientist or whatever?"

"Mia, just get out of here," gabbled Danny. "Don't come back! Don't ever come back!"

The bald man looked at Mia and smiled. A thought seemed to pass from his head and into Danny's. *If you press Pause, what will happen when you press Play? I'll still be here with your sister. If you press Rewind and then Play, I'll still come to the house tonight and if you're not here, you'll never see your sister again.*

"Danny," whispered Mia. "None of the lights work, so I brought my torch."

Then Danny noticed something strange. The bald man froze. A look of genuine fear crossed his face.

"Torch," he hissed.

Mia flicked her torch on and swung the beam round so that it pointed down into the hall.

She located Danny and said, "I thought you were sleeping in the washing machine."

She swung the beam towards the front door. It swept over the bald man's neck and, as it did, it cut straight into his skin and left a thick red stripe under his chin.

"Drat!" the bald man roared, clutching his neck in pain.

"Hubert! Arthur! Montgomery! Grab that torch!" he barked.

The robot mice scuttled down his body and across the carpet. Mia watched them curiously as they hopped up the stairs towards her.

"What peculiar creatures," she sniffed as she lifted up her foot.

There was a CRUNCH as she trod on the first mouse, then a CRACK as she stamped on the second mouse and a SQUELCH as she squashed the third.

"N-no," stammered the bald man. "My – rodents!"

"Mia, point the torch at him again!" Danny called out. "It's like he can't stand bright light."

"Oh I see," said Mia. "Righty-ho."

She pointed the torch directly at the bald man. As it crossed his body, it seemed to score a line across his chest, *through* his shirt. He was so sensitive to light that even his clothes couldn't protect him.

"Curses – should – have – put on – special suit," groaned the bald man, staggering backwards in agony.

Mia moved the torch in zigzags down his legs, making him hop from one foot to the other.

Finally she trained the torch on his face.

"And – should – have – put on – special – cream," hissed the bald man.

His skin grew redder and redder, slowly turning brown and then purple. Sweat streamed down his face and steam poured off his head.

"I'll come back," he spat. "I'll find you – I'll find both of you..."

He turned round and fled. A fourth robot mouse fell out of his pocket with a clunk and, after a brief glassy look at Danny and Mia, it scuttled away after its master.

Danny and Mia stared at the front door for a few seconds, half expecting the bald man – or one of his mice – to come back.

Then Danny strode across to the light switch in the hall. He tried turning it on.

"He really did shut down all the power in the house," murmured Danny.

"Did you see the way the torch hurt him through his clothes?" said Mia. "How bizarre was that?"

There was a sudden bump in their parents' bedroom. A door opened upstairs and their mother started hissing instructions to their father.

"Danny, you'd better get out of here," said Mia. "They'll go mad if they find you down here."

Danny nodded. "Thanks."

"Here," said Mia. "Take this. The light seemed to hurt him."

She held up the torch.

Danny shook his head. "No. You keep it. In case he comes back here. I've got my remote and next time I'll use it on him."

Danny brandished his remote like a sword.

Mr and Mrs Danger began to creep down the stairs, whispering to each other.

"I'm telling you, there's someone down here," said Mrs Danger.

"You're imagining things," replied Mr Danger.

"I bet they've trodden mud into my carpets," said Mrs Danger, "and ruined my lovely clean kitchen."

But when Mr and Mrs Danger reached the hallway, there was nobody there.

Danny ran up the front garden and into the street.

He glanced left and right, scanning his surroundings for a bald head, yellow eyes, a white coat.

He remembered Mia saying, "The light seemed to hurt him," and he ran towards the nearest streetlight.

When he reached the lamp post, he glanced around for any signs of movement, but there was nothing.

He decided to stay close to the streetlights, reasoning that they were like giant torches and would hopefully stop the bald man from approaching.

He walked along the pavement. After a few minutes, the light from one lamp post ran out. There was a strip of darkness and then the light from the next lamp post began.

The strip of darkness seemed to throb and pulse. It felt like a black river or a dark pit that Danny had to leap over without falling into. He imagined hands waiting there in the darkness, hands waiting to pull him down, to drag him away.

He took a deep breath. He sprinted across the patch of darkness, the air roaring in his ears, pulling at his clothes and whipping round his feet.

He bounded into the next pool of light, slowing down gradually as he reached the centre.

Using this method, he made his way along the street, dashing from one lamp post to the next, tearing across stretches of darkness and lingering in patches of light.

Then, at the end of the street, there was a problem. A streetlight flickering on, off, on, off. One moment it lit up the pavement, the next it plunged that part of the street into total darkness.

He wasn't sure if he imagined a pair of yellow eyes waiting for him in the shadows.

The streetlight flickered on again, revealing nothing but an empty pavement.

Danny looked down at his remote. He had almost forgotten it was in his hand, ready to use. He placed his thumb on the Pause button.

But something stopped him from pressing it. He realised that he wanted to know what would happen next. It might be dangerous, it might be frightening, but he wanted to be around when it happened.

So he looked again at the light flickering under the lamp post. It was time to decide whether to push ahead or change direction.

At that moment, he saw Eric's house at the end of the street, just beyond the flickering lamp post. Of course! He wasn't sure if Eric would be back from his Auntie Gladys's, but his house would still be the safest place for Danny.

He waited till the light flashed on, and darted forwards as quickly as he could. He was halfway through when he felt the light trembling, so he forced himself to run even faster. A split second later he was out the other side, across the tiny strip of darkness, and panting beside the next lamp post down, safe in a solid column of brightness. After getting his breath back, he sprinted over to Eric's house, rushing even more determinedly from one circle of light to the next.

He was relieved to find that there was a lamp post outside Eric's house. Even better, when he walked towards the house, a security light immediately pinged on, bathing the front lawn in a yellow glow. Danny took his usual route into the house, clambering on the extension roof and pulling Eric's window open.

In the darkness of Eric's room, Danny saw that his friend was lying in his bed, fast asleep.

It didn't matter. Danny felt better already.

He lay down on the floor next to Eric's bed and stared up at the ceiling.

He would wait a few hours till Eric woke up and then talk to him about the cosmic remote, his Uncle Charlie, the bald man and what he should do next.

He lay there, telling himself it would be safer if he stayed awake.

Less than a minute later, he was asleep.

Outside in the street, a cat sat quietly underneath a parked car. It stared up at Eric's house with glittering red eyes while the felt on its body rose and fell with a soft mechanical purr.

6
PAUSE

When Danny woke up, it was dawn.

Sunlight streamed into the bedroom through a gap in the curtains, making everything – Eric's books and toys and posters – twinkle with life.

Danny could sense the remote lying on his chest. He had felt sure that nobody would catch him or attack him in Eric's house. Happily his instincts had been right.

Memories from the night before flooded into his head. For a few moments, his heart beat faster as he thought about his uncle and Mia and the bald man and the electronic mice.

He wondered if he could rewind the past

twenty-four hours and make everything different – find his uncle, warn his sister and hand out torches. They could fight the bald man side by side.

Eric's voice brought him back to the present.

"All right, Danny?" said Eric. "What you doing here?"

"Oh, hi Eric," said Danny with a dazed smile.

"Did your mum actually throw you out?" Eric asked, sitting up in his bed.

"No," said Danny. "Nothing like that." He looked down at the remote. "It's about this remote control. It's got cosmic powers. It can move time around. You know, stop it, move it backwards and forwards. I got it from my uncle. Seems he works for some secret gadget police or something. And now this old bald man's chasing me, trying to take it off me."

Eric looked blank while he took all of this in. Then an amazed smile spread across his face.

"Wow!" he exclaimed. "Show us how it works."

"OK," said Danny. He was about to press Pause when he noticed that the Play button was flashing.

"That's odd," said Danny. "It's never done that before."

"What is it?" said Eric. "Are we about to get rewound? Or paused? That must feel so weird."

Danny pressed Play and two shapes shot out of the end of the remote.

One was a young man with spiky hair, thick-rimmed glasses and a massive pair of headphones round his neck. The other was a young woman with dyed pink hair, glittery make-up and fluorescent green leggings.

"Hi," said the young man. "I'm Jasper."

"And I'm Roxie," said the young woman.

"You're clearly using your remote for something else at the moment, so we'll leave a message," said Jasper.

The outlines of Jasper and Roxie flickered and then stabilised. Eric stared at them with his mouth wide open.

"Your uncle asked us to come," said Roxie. "EUREKA! agents have to watch each other's backs, you know. He gave us this letter to deliver."

"Yeah," said Jasper, pulling two sheets of paper out of his pocket. "Don't know why he didn't want us to email it. Could have used my new air slate, it's got this incredible—"

"Jasper," said Roxie. "Just deliver the letter."

"But the air slate's amazing," protested Jasper. "You just speak to it and the words appear in mid-air."

"Yeah, I know," said Roxie. "I've had one for like nine months. Jeez, Jasper, you can move things around with your *mind*, you don't need half these gadgets anyway. Just do what Charlie asked and give Danny his letter."

"Fine, whatever," said Jasper. "Let's mince some molecules."

He held the letter in his right hand, closed his eyes and flicked it through the air towards Danny.

When it was halfway between Jasper and Danny, something unusual happened. When it was closer to Jasper, it was still a recording, a matrix of colour and light produced by the cosmic remote, wavering and shimmering like Jasper and Roxie. When the letter was falling towards Danny's feet, it began to look denser, its corners grew sharper, its colour was more defined and the ink on its pages grew darker and clearer. It began to look like everything else in Eric's room. By the time it landed on the floor it became an ordinary common-or-garden letter, no different from the kind of letter that you would get through your door – you could pick it up, turn it over, fold it up.

Danny and Eric stared at it for a few seconds.

"Way to go, Jasper!" exclaimed Roxie. "The

package has arrived at its destination!"

"Right, can I show them the air slate now?" asked Jasper. "Or at least my wind skimmer?"

"The Professor confiscated your wind skimmer because you hit a pigeon with it," sighed Roxie. "Besides, Danny's got to open his letter." She looked straight ahead. "Read the note as quickly as you can, Danny. And remember – you've got a lot of friends at EUREKA!"

Jasper and Roxie flickered, faded and finally fizzled out.

Eric was the first to speak. "Wow, your gadget is amazing."

"I didn't even know it could do that," said Danny.

"Aren't you going to read the letter then?" asked Eric.

"Yeah," said Danny. "I suppose I should."

"Let me read it over your shoulder," begged Eric.

So Danny picked up the two sheets of paper and the two boys read the letter.

First, there was a note from Danny's uncle. It read:

Sorry I got you into this, Dan. I'm on my way, but in the meantime, here's what you need to know.

Then there was a sheet of paper that Uncle Charlie had clearly ripped out of a textbook.

THE EUREKA! HANDBOOK

some say that this magical pig has the ability to sing like a budgerigar.

THE NIGHT SCIENTIST: Born Herbert Perkins, 1939. Perkins began his career as a scientist at S.M.A.R.T. (Society for the Massively Ambitious and Ridiculously Talented). Perkins was originally working on a cure for Owwdat-Hertz disease, but he grew more interested in obscurer forms of knowledge.

First, he tried to manufacture a drug that would make him live for ever. However when he tested it on a group of mice, they turned blue, their tails dropped off and then they exploded. Next, he was convinced he'd invented a drug that made humans invisible. However when he gave it to a pair of rats, they became invisible for a few seconds — but then they exploded too. In fact, all of his drugs had this unfortunate side effect. You could grow wings and fly, you could see into other people's minds, you could run faster than a cheetah, provided you didn't mind exploding a few minutes later.

But none of this discouraged Perkins. The more setbacks he encountered, the more determined he became to discover something that would win him fame, power and money. He began to work around the clock, rarely leaving his laboratory, sleeping for a few hours in the afternoon. This caused a dramatic change in his appearance. Without sunlight, his skin grew paler and paler and his hair became crinkly and eventually fell out. His eyes began to look like a nocturnal animal's:

bright yellow with large black pupils. Soon he found that he couldn't go out during the day, as the sunlight hurt his eyes and burned his skin. It was around this time that he began to be known as "the Night Scientist".

It was also around this time that he built his first robot animal. Although he couldn't bear the sunlight, he realised that he still needed to go outside to buy food or to find chemicals for his experiments. He built a small remote-controlled shrew that could run errands for him during the day. When the (robot) shrew was eaten by a (real) fox, he built another shrew and a robot Alsatian to defend it against foxes. When the Alsatian malfunctioned and also ate the shrew, the Night Scientist decided to make his animals harder to digest or destroy, giving them stronger skeletons, denser fur, sharper teeth and claws. Within a few months, his robot army was complete. He had dozens of fish, birds, insects and mammals — all ready to brave the sunlight for him, all built to last for ever, all trained to respond to his voice and no one else's.

For all of these reasons, the Night Scientist should be regarded as highly dangerous. As the years have passed, his desire for power and knowledge has become stronger than ever. His experiments continue to fail so he preys on other scientists and researchers, stealing their ideas and inventions.

If he approaches you, politely explain that you are late for school or work and walk away at a brisk pace. If he seems bent on combat, stand your ground as best you can and remember that he cannot tolerate light or sunshine. It is said that even a domestic torch can produce enough light to hurt him.

The Night's Scientist's current obsession is time travel.

"Now I get it!" murmured Danny. "Why he turned off the electricity in our house. Why Mia's torch burned him. And why he wants to get his hands on my remote."

"You're saying this guy's real?" asked Eric.

"He's the one who's been setting all these robot animals on me," said Danny. "He's the one who broke into my house last night."

"Flippin' 'eck," said Eric.

"But what's happened to Uncle Charlie? Why didn't those two people tell me?" lamented Danny.

Eric spent a few seconds looking at the remote in Danny's hand.

"Hey, listen," he said. "If people can contact you through the remote, then maybe you can use it to get in touch with your uncle."

Danny looked at Eric and then down at the remote.

"Maybe. But I don't know how to make it send messages," said Danny.

"I'll have a try if you like!" said Eric, hopefully.

"No!" cried Danny, and clutched the remote tightly to his chest.

There was an awkward few seconds, as Danny stared into space and Eric played sheepishly with his toys.

Eric picked up his remote-controlled robot and fiddled with one of the arms.

"Look, sorry, I lost it a bit there," said Danny apologetically. "It's been a weird few days. Hey, Eric, why don't I show you what the remote can do? It's not like this Night Scientist bloke is going to be after me during the day."

"Cool!" replied Eric cheerfully.

"Shall I pause time first?" asked Danny.

"Yes, definitely!" said Eric.

"So you see that robot in your hand?" said Danny. "I'm going to pause time, take it out of your hand and put it on your desk. So you'll just be aware of the robot vanishing from your hand and reappearing on the desk. OK?"

"Fantastic!" said Eric, trembling very slightly.

Danny pressed Pause and put the robot on

Eric's desk. He stood in front of Eric again and pressed Play.

Eric came back to life and flinched. He flexed his fingers, but there was no robot in his hand. There it was on his desk.

He looked stunned and then delighted. "That is the best thing ever!"

"Now I'm going to rewind time," said Danny. "So look, you have to concentrate on this moment, because you're not going to remember anything from now on."

"OK," said Eric, frowning hard, trying to concentrate as much as he could.

"I'm going to get something from the future and bring it back to this point in time," explained Danny.

"Got it." Eric nodded, still frowning.

"So let's write a letter," said Danny, moving across to Eric's desk.

Eric followed him. "What do you mean?"

"Here you are," said Danny, handing Eric a pen. "Write yourself a letter from the future."

Eric took the pen and said: "Wow!" He

picked up a piece of paper from the desk.

After holding the pen a few centimetres above the piece of paper for two minutes, he said: "What shall I write?"

"Anything," said Danny.

"OK," said Eric. He scratched his head and bit the end of the pen. Finally he wrote:

Hi Eric. This is Eric. I'm writing from the future. How cool is that?

"Write down something that nobody knows but you. To prove it's really you," suggested Danny.

Eric wrote:

You've hidden two Mars Bars in your sock drawer.

"OK, great," said Danny. He took the letter from Eric and folded it in half.

Then he pressed Rewind. He watched Eric unwriting the letter although the paper itself wasn't there – it was just the pen hoovering up the ink. Then when Eric had scampered backwards into the middle of the room, Danny pressed Play.

Eric did a double take as Danny was suddenly standing in a different part of the room.

"Here," said Danny, striding towards Eric with the letter in his hand.

Eric started to read.

"You wrote it in the future," said Danny. "Of course, it's not the future any more," he added.

When Eric had finished reading, his eyes were glazed and his mouth was wide open.

"It's no wonder that the Night Scientist wants your remote," he said. "It's absolutely amazing. Hey, you know what you could do. You could be like a superhero. Helping people out when they're in trouble. You know, say you see someone falling off a building. You could pause time, fetch a big mattress, push the mattress into place, press Play, and – hey presto – the person lands on the mattress."

"Yeah –" said Danny, with a smile.

"Hey! That's what we should do today," Eric continued. "We should go round town, helping people. You know, when something bad happens, you rewind time and try to stop it. It'll be brilliant!"

Danny thought about this. It would certainly be more fun than hiding in a tree somewhere, waiting for Uncle Charlie to call.

"OK," he said.

Eric cheered. "Let's head for the high street," he said. "It's Sunday so it'll be pretty busy."

"Sure," said Danny.

Eric picked up his robot. "I'm going to take Magnus with me. He'll definitely want to see this!"

Danny and Eric walked to the end of their street, turned right and headed towards the town centre. Danny told Eric a bit more about the things he had done with his remote: pausing his parents, recording his sister, rewinding his teacher.

They had only been walking for five minutes when Eric saw an old lady who was trying to cross a busy road.

"Hey, look at her," he said. "Why not press Pause, stop all the cars and move her across the road?"

Danny looked up at the traffic. "It might freak her out. You know, suddenly appearing on the other side of the street?"

Eric replied, "She'll be OK. She's old, isn't she? She'll just think it's one of those things."

Danny smiled. "All right," he said.

He pressed Pause and everything froze.

He walked over to the old lady and tugged her sleeve, just to check she couldn't see or feel anything. At the same time, he realised that he had never tried to move an actual person when they were paused. He wondered if it would be the same as moving an object.

Danny stood alongside the old lady and put his arms round her waist. He tried lifting her straight up, but she didn't budge. He leaned back and tried again, but she still wouldn't move. Finally, he bent his legs and heaved with all his might. She moved, slowly at first, and then more quickly. It was like pulling a plant up by the roots.

Danny decided that people must be more securely fixed in time than objects, and much harder to wrench out of place.

That said, now the old lady was off the ground, she was surprisingly light. Danny looked across the street and saw that there was a clear line to the other side of the road, in between the frozen cars and motorbikes.

He lifted the old lady up as high as he could, so she was like a rolled-up carpet resting on his shoulder. Then he ran towards the opposite kerb, tottering wildly, moving quickly, then slowly, then forwards, then backwards, until he reached the other side of the road and put her down with an awkward plonk. The old lady wobbled for a few seconds, then settled into her place.

He ran back across the street and stood next to Eric. He pressed Play.

Eric came back to life. "Wow! You did it!' he exclaimed.

The old lady looked up in surprise, then shrugged, and shuffled off down the road.

"See, I told you she'd take it in her stride," said Eric. "Come on, let's help someone else."

They reached the high street five minutes later. The shops had just opened, and the pavements were already full of people.

"Look over there," said Eric, pointing across to the other side of the street.

A woman was struggling down the road with a large birthday cake balanced in her arms. She tripped on a paving stone, the cake flew though the air, flipped over twice and landed with a whoomph on a man coming out of a shop. The man looked stunned for a few seconds, then quietly began to wipe cake out of his eyes, pull it out of his hair and brush it off his shoulders. He pulled a birthday candle out of his nose.

The woman stammered at the man, "I'm so sorry. I'm so sorry." She whimpered to herself, "My daughter's cake. My daughter's cake."

"Hey, you catch the cake," said Eric. "I'll get the man out of the way."

"OK," said Danny with a smile. He pressed Rewind and then Play.

Eric and he were about to turn into the high street.

"Eric," said Danny. "See that woman carrying a cake over there? In about thirty seconds she's going to trip over and she'll throw the cake at a man coming out of a shop. You have to get the man out of the way, I'll catch the cake.

"This was your idea by the way," he added.

"Cool, so you just rewound everything?" Eric asked.

Danny nodded.

The two boys scampered across the road.

They walked in step with the lady carrying the cake for a few seconds and then, when she tripped, Eric ran one way and Danny ran the other. Eric leapt into the shop doorway and pushed the man out of the way.

"What in heaven's name...?" the man exclaimed, but then he realised what was happening.

Danny was standing underneath the cake, moving a little to the left, then a little to the right.

The cake twirled through the air. He took a few steps backwards and moved his legs apart so they were planted firmly on the ground. The cake was plummeting fast. Danny held his arms straight out in front of him and closed his eyes. The cake dropped like a stone and landed neatly in Danny's outstretched arms, sending a little cloud of icing sugar up into the air and squirting a small blob of cream on to the pavement.

"Oh, thank you, boys, thank you," said the woman.

"Yes, well done, lads," said the man. "Well spotted. You must have eyes like a hawk."

"No problem, mister," said Eric.

Danny handed the birthday cake to the lady, straightening one of the candles. "There you go," he said.

Eric and Danny walked away, grinning broadly.

"This is great," said Eric. "We'll soon be the most popular boys in town!"

"I wonder if there'll be any other accidents like that," said Danny. "It's not like people throw cakes around every day."

"Something will happen," said Eric. "Grown-ups are always falling over and dropping things. Haven't you noticed?"

Just as Danny was about to answer, a strange sequence of events unfolded. A man opened the door of his car into the road. A woman on a bike swerved to avoid him and ended up riding on to the pavement. A flock of pigeons flew out of her way, straight into the path of a young man pushing an old man in a wheelchair. The young man let go of the wheelchair to bat the pigeons out of his eyes. The wheelchair trundled down the pavement and headed for a group of workmen who were digging a hole in the road. One of the workmen turned round just as he was knocked into the hole by the wheelchair.

The workman landed on a water pipe at the bottom of the hole, breaking it open and sending a jet of white spray into the air. This hit the bottom of the wheelchair. The old man clung on tightly as he was lifted ten metres off the ground. He landed with a clunk on top of a passing van, which veered off the road and hit a tree. The tree toppled over and crashed through the roof of the local church. Beams and bricks from the roof dropped on to the pavement and knocked over a set of traffic lights. Cars began to shunt into each other, a shop window shattered and fire-engine sirens wailed in the distance.

"Blimey," said Danny, blinking in disbelief.

"It's lucky we're here," said Eric, staring at the church roof.

"Really lucky," said Danny.

"Unbelievably lucky," he added, as an old lady ran screaming past them.

Danny pressed Rewind. He walked over to the shop where Eric and he had caught the cake. When Eric was in position, he pressed Play.

"—we'll soon be the most popular boys in town," Eric was saying.

"Hey, Eric, you're never going to believe this," said Danny. He explained to Eric how a man was going to open a car door and cause a bike to veer off course and soon the whole high street would be a disaster area.

"Wow," said Eric. "Part of me *really* wants to see that."

"It's pretty grim though," said Danny.

"So all we have to do is stop *that man* opening his car door?" said Eric.

Danny nodded.

Eric ran over to the car and tapped on the passenger door window.

The man in the car frowned, leaned over and wound down the window.

"Be careful when you open your door, mister," said Eric.

"Why of course I will, you cheeky rascal!" the man huffed.

He turned round and went to open his door. A cyclist whipped past him.

"See what I mean," said Eric.

"Mmm, yes, I suppose that was close," the man muttered. "Cyclists are such a nuisance," he added, as if it wasn't really his fault after all.

Eric returned to Danny's side. All was calm and quiet on the high street.

"If only they knew, eh?" Eric said.

7
STOP

"Let's keep helping people," said Eric. "We can make sure nothing bad ever happens. It'll be brilliant."

At that point, his face fell.

"What's up?" Danny asked.

Eric nodded towards the newsagent's. Mia had just walked out.

"Oh, it's OK," said Danny. "I don't mind Mia at the moment."

"You don't mind her?" asked Eric.

Danny explained. "No, she really helped out last night, when the Night Scientist attacked me. You remember I told you about her coming downstairs with the torch."

"Oh. Right," replied Eric, unconvinced.

Mia walked over to where Danny and Eric were standing. She gave Eric a weak smile.

"You OK?" she asked Danny.

"Yeah," said Danny. "You OK?"

"Mmm," said Mia.

"I told Eric," said Danny. "You know, about the remote, and the man attacking us and everything."

"Oh, OK," said Mia.

Danny told Mia about the letter from Roxie and Jasper and what he had discovered about the Night Scientist.

"Shouldn't you be somewhere safe?" said Mia. "Instead of out in broad daylight?"

"I don't think the Night Scientist will show his face until, er, night," said Danny. "Anyway, guess what? Me and Eric are helping people. We just caught a cake. And stopped a tree from falling down."

"What do you mean?" asked Mia.

So Danny told Mia about how they had

paused time, and rewound time, and stopped bad things from happening.

"That does sound pretty cool," she admitted.

"You're not going to let her join in, are you?" whispered Eric.

Mia scowled at Eric.

"She *is* my sister," said Danny.

"But she's mean," said Eric. "*Really* mean."

"She's changed," said Danny. "Haven't you, Mia?"

Mia shrugged. "Not massively," she said.

"I told you!" said Eric.

"Look, don't worry about it," said Mia. "If I'd wanted to hang out with nerds in my spare time, I'd have joined the chess club. Danny, I'll see you at home maybe."

Danny nodded. "OK," he said. "Bye."

As Mia walked away, Eric exclaimed, "Look at this massive puddle, Danny."

Danny turned round.

"That bus is heading straight for it. All those people are going to get soaked," said Eric.

Sure enough, a bus ploughed through a puddle in the road, sending a sheet of water on to the pavement and drenching half a dozen people that were queuing outside the baker's.

"Press Rewind and warn them!" Eric said.

"Oh – yeah," mumbled Danny, gathering his thoughts. "OK."

However, before Danny had the chance to press Rewind, he heard footsteps behind him and felt an arm grabbing his shoulder. It was Mia.

"Danny, up there!" she said breathlessly, pointing up at the sky.

Danny looked up and saw a flock of birds hovering below the clouds. He was about to ask Mia what the problem was, when he noticed that they seemed to be parrots and toucans, with bright multicoloured plumage and curved beaks.

"Something funny's going on," said Mia. "There's no way you'd normally see birds like that in England."

The birds seemed to be descending.

"It's got to be the Night Scientist," said Mia. "You know, like the mice from last night. And the fish you saw in the park. Those birds can't be real."

"Crumbs," said Eric.

"Let's walk as quickly as we can back to the house," said Mia.

"Let's go to my house," suggested Eric. "My parents aren't mad like yours."

"OK, fine," said Mia. "But let's go."

They strode down the high street as quickly as they could.

Eric glanced sadly at a cat stuck up a tree, regretting that they couldn't stop and help – just for a minute or two. Then he spotted a man chasing after a bus – it was a shame they couldn't Rewind time and help him too.

But Mia was right – the birds did look strange. They'd have to help people later.

The three children turned left off the high street. The birds seemed to swerve to the left too. The three children began to walk more quickly. The birds began to flap their wings more strongly too.

In fact, whenever the children made a movement on the ground – turning left or right, going up a hill or following a footpath, the birds seemed to imitate them, tilting gently to one side or the other, dropping or rising slightly.

The three children turned into their street. Eric's house was on the right, Danny and Mia's was further down the road on the left.

"OK," said Mia. "Into Eric's house."

"Mia," said Danny.

"We'll hide out till they've gone," said Mia.

"Mia!" said Danny.

"What is it?" asked Mia impatiently.

"Look," said Danny, and pointed straight ahead.

There, in the middle of the road, the birds had landed. They were six metallic parrots, with glittering crystal eyes, fibreglass feathers and iron claws, all standing perfectly still as if they were waiting for orders.

Nobody moved.

Then Eric whispered, "I've got an idea."

"Don't do anything," hissed Mia.

"It'll be OK, watch," said Eric.

All the time they had been in town, he had had his home-made robot, Magnus, tucked under his arm. Now he put it on the ground and whispered, "Straight ahead."

The robot trundled out into the road and headed for the parrots. When it was within two metres of the birds, Eric called out: "Stop."

The robot stopped.

"Now fire," said Eric.

The robot lifted up its right arm. It was holding a small water pistol. It squirted a jet of water at one of the parrots.

All six of the birds suddenly came to life. They swarmed over the robot, pecking and flapping, clambering over each other and shoving each other out of the way. Then they all returned to their original positions, standing in the road, staring straight ahead, not moving, not making a sound.

The robot was a pile of cogs, metal splinters and grey dust.

"Magnus!" exclaimed Eric.

"Eric, no!" Danny cried, holding Eric back when his friend tried to run out into the road.

"Look what they've done to Magnus!" said Eric.

"We'll – we'll – repair him later," said Danny.

"Repair him?" exclaimed Eric. "There's nothing left to repair."

"At least we know not to try and fight them," said Mia. "They're too powerful for us."

Danny still clung on to Eric. "What shall we do then?" he said to Mia.

"Use your remote," she said. "Take it out of your pocket very slowly. Press Pause. Get something out of Dad's shed, like a hammer maybe, and knock them for six."

Danny nodded.

"Can't you rewind time first?" pleaded Eric. "And bring Magnus back?"

"Who cares about your stupid robot?" said Mia. "Danny, just get rid of those birds."

"Danny, don't listen to her," said Eric. "You only have to Rewind a couple of minutes. Then Pause."

"What's the point of bringing your robot back?" sneered Mia. "It hardly put up much of a fight, did it?"

"You take that back, you big meanie," wailed Eric.

"Shh," hissed Danny. "Shh. Look."

Eric and Mia looked up. The birds had vanished.

"Where did they go?" snapped Mia.

"I don't know. I was distracted by you two bickering," said Danny.

Then they all felt themselves lifted straight up into the air. The ground was ten, twenty, thirty, forty, fifty metres away.

They were above the clouds

before they realised what had happened.

The parrots had swept them into the sky. Each of the children had one parrot clinging to their left shoulder and one parrot clinging to their right shoulder.

The parrots were now flying straight ahead, their eyes glittering and their feathers rippling.

"You're coming with us! You're coming with us!" they squawked.

Mia was the first to pull herself together.

"Danny, press Rewind!" she called out.

"You're coming with us! You're coming with us!" the parrots squawked again.

"Danny! Rewind! Now!" cried Mia.

"You're coming with us! You're coming with us!" repeated the parrots.

Danny was in a trance. The wind in his face was making his eyes water – or maybe he was crying? The currents of air were making his clothes flutter – or maybe he was shaking?

He half heard Mia's words and tried to put his hand in his pocket.

But the parrots were clinging tightly to his

shoulders. He could barely move his arms: they were wrenched halfway up his body and dangled uselessly by his sides.

"Rewind!" yelled Mia.

Eric had come to. "Rewind!" he called out.

"Can't!" spluttered Danny. "Parrots! My arms!"

Mia seemed to realise what had happened and stopped calling out. But Eric whimpered "Rewind!" for another five minutes.

"They're going to drop us," Danny said out loud. "And not even my remote can save us."

"If they were going to drop us, they'd have done it by now," said Mia.

The parrots dropped them.

As they fell, Danny instinctively felt for his remote. He managed to press Pause.

He realised that Mia and Eric had frozen in mid-air, but he was still falling, so he flung out his left arm and managed to grab hold of Eric's right ankle. Eric stayed fixed in place for a second or two, but then he started to judder and tilt. Danny threw his right arm towards Mia and grabbed her shin. Both Eric and Mia dropped a centimetre and then half a centimetre. Then they stopped dead.

Danny breathed out and closed his eyes. It seemed that, together, Eric and Mia could support his weight. He kept his eyes closed, trying to detect any further movement. But there was none. He was safe for now.

Danny's eyes flicked open when his remote rang. He quickly let go of Eric and reached into his pocket. He pulled out his remote and noticed the Play button was flashing.

If he pushed it, would they all start falling again?

But there was no time to lose; Mia was beginning to shake. He pressed Play and held the remote between his teeth.

He recognised the voice immediately.

"You find yourself on what some people call 'the horns of a dilemma'," drawled the Night Scientist.

"I'm – I'm not afraid of you," spluttered Danny.

But the Night Scientist kept talking and

Danny realised that the voice was a recording.

"You must realise that the only way I can have left this message is because I know your remote's unique code locator. And that is how I know your exact location." The Night Scientist continued, "You're 1009.3 metres above the ground."

Danny glanced quickly down at the clouds below him.

"So let's review the situation," said the Night Scientist. "I would imagine that you've pressed Pause. You're probably clinging on to your friend's leg or your sister's leg or both. Perhaps you're holding the remote in your mouth, like a dog with a bone. Next, you'll try Rewind."

Danny mumbled, "Oh yeah, good idea," and stared down at the remote in his mouth.

"But ask yourself this," went on the Night Scientist. "How long do you press Rewind for? A minute? Two minutes? Till you're back on the ground? Till you're back on the high street?"

The voice cackled.

"However far back you rewind, you'll never

stop me finding you. You see, I first heard about the cosmic remote in 1982, years before you were born. Do you see? So to stop me knowing about the remote, to stop me wanting the remote, you'd have to rewind time till – well – 1981 at the very least. Do you think you can pull *that* off? Think you've got it in you, Daniel, hmm?"

The voice cackled again.

"What I'm trying to say is: you have to face me sometime. You can't keep running away. You know I'm not going to give up my quest for the remote. Not after thirty years. So here's what you should do."

Danny's brain was racing. He got ready to let go of Mia's leg and press Rewind.

"You allow yourself to fall," said the Night Scientist. "The parrots have been programmed to drop you at an exact point in time and space. You'll fall for about thirty seconds. You'll look down and see a barn in a field rising to meet you. Don't worry. You're going to fall through an open hatch in the roof. You'll all land on gigantic hay bales which will break your fall. You may suffer a few cuts and bruises – nothing more. You will then wait in the barn till nightfall when I will come and speak with you. As you have no doubt realised, I'm not at my best during the daytime."

Danny glanced up at Mia's twisted face. She looked terrified.

"Of course, I've taken a few precautions. The barn is locked. There's no way out. There's no way in. Naturally you can use your remote – in which case I'll see you tomorrow, or the day after that, or the day after that."

The voice crackled and went dead.

He's lying, said Danny to himself. *If I press Play, we'll all splatter on the ground.*

Then another thought crossed his mind.

But if I hit the ground, so will the remote. It will break into a thousand pieces. He won't want that.

Then he seemed to make a decision.

What choice do I have? Do I stay up here for the rest of my life?

He let go of Eric's leg, grabbed the remote

out of his mouth and pressed Play. The wind roared in his ears and he heard Eric and Mia yelling.

"We're going to be OK. We're going to be OK," Danny tried to say, but the wind rushed over his face so quickly that his lips vibrated and his cheeks flapped and he ended up just slobbering.

He shot through the hatch in the barn roof and landed on the haystack with a crunch. Mia landed behind him and Eric landed next to him. The haystack shook and squeaked for a few seconds. They lay on their backs for five minutes, not saying a word, just breathing deeply and thinking.

"We're alive," said Mia finally.

"Are we?" asked Eric.

"OK, you can press

Rewind now, Danny," said Mia.

"Hang on a minute," said Eric. "That was mind-blowing. I don't ever want to forget that."

"Don't be ridiculous," said Mia. "It was terrifying. Besides, where are we?" She sat up. "In a barn Goodness Knows Where. Danny, please. Rewind. Now."

"Can't we at least see where we are first," asked Eric. He bounced down off the haystack, on to the floor of the barn.

"The door will be locked, Eric," said Danny flatly.

Eric went over to the barn door. He rattled it a few times. It was locked tight.

Mia gave Danny a strange look.

"OK, Danny, what's going on?" she asked.

"Right, now don't panic," said Danny. "Hear me out."

He explained how he had paused time and what the Night Scientist had said.

It took a few seconds for it to sink in, and then Eric said: "OK, I agree with Mia now. Press Rewind."

"Hang on," said Mia. "I've changed my mind too. The Night Scientist may be a nasty piece of work, but he's right. You do have to confront him."

"N-no," stammered Eric. "No you don't."

"As soon as he gets here," said Mia, "you should press Pause. Then bash him on the head. Teach him a lesson once and for all."

"Don't listen to her!" exclaimed Eric. "This Night Scientist bloke is as evil as it gets. You remember the letter from your uncle. He's highly dangerous. He'll take the remote and leave us here to rot."

"He can't take the remote without Danny letting him," said Mia. "Danny can just press Pause and stop him. Or press Rewind and stop him."

"You saw what he did to Magnus," said Eric. "He'll do the same to us."

Eric and Mia both fell silent, looking up at Danny every few seconds.

Danny finally said, "I want to face him."

"No!" Eric cried. "You can't listen to a girl.

Girls don't know anything."

"I'm not doing it because of Mia," said Danny. "I think I have to do it. That's all."

"Danny. Look, give me the remote. I'll press Rewind if you don't want to," said Eric.

Mia stood in front of Danny and folded her arms.

"Oi," she said.

Eric sat down on the edge of a hay bale and put his head in his hands.

"I can't believe I'm here. Maybe this is all a bad dream. Maybe I'll wake up in my room with all my things. Mum and Dad will come in and say: 'Let's go to the park!' I'll spend the afternoon on the swings. OK, I'm going to wake up now. One, two, three. Wake up!" He sat up and opened his eyes wide.

"One, two, three. Wake up!" he said again.

He opened his eyes even wider.

"Flippin' 'eck!" Eric sighed and put his head in his hands again.

They didn't say much for the rest of the day. They patiently waited for night to come.

Every hour or so, Eric would try another line of argument.

"My parents will be so worried."

"After all I've done for you, can't you do this for me?"

"Just Rewind us back to the high street. Then you and Mia can be kidnapped by the birds and I'll stay behind."

By five in the evening Eric realised it was pointless, and he gave up and sat in a distant corner of the barn by himself.

Danny was staring into space, thinking. He had wanted to face the Night Scientist, but he wanted to make sure he was in control when it happened.

Slowly but surely, a plan formed in his head.

Just before sunset, he called Mia and Eric over to where he was sitting.

"What do you want?" Eric huffed.

"What's up, Danny?" asked Mia.

"I think I've worked out what we should do," said Danny. "Eric, you know how you don't want to be here? Well, maybe you shouldn't be here. Maybe none of us should be here."

"What do you mean?" mumbled Eric.

"Mia, you remember how last night I recorded lots of versions of myself – to put the Night Scientist off?" said Danny. "Well, how about I record nothing? Just one side of the barn? Then we can all hide behind it."

Mia frowned. "You're not making any sense, Danny."

"It's easier if I show you," he said, and placed his remote on a hay bale. He pressed Record and light covered the far end of the barn.

"I still don't understand," said Eric.

"Just wait," said Danny. He waited till a minute had passed, then pressed Stop.

"Now look," said Danny.

He pressed Play and a recording of the far end of the barn shot out of the remote. He balanced the remote on the hay bale, turning it until the edges of the recording and the edges of the actual barn lined up exactly. You couldn't tell where the real barn ended and the recording started.

"Watch this," said Danny. He ran towards the recorded image, running through it as if it were a waterfall. Eric and Mia watched in disbelief. Danny had been swallowed up by the barn wall.

"Danny?" Mia called out after a few seconds.

Danny stuck his head through the recorded image. It looked as if his head was floating in mid air.

"See what I mean?" said Danny's head. "I record one end of the barn. Then I press Play. Then we can all hide behind the recording."

Mia suddenly understood and she smiled.

Danny emerged from behind the recording. He balanced the remote on the hay bale again, and pressed Record.

"I just need to record a good chunk of time," said Danny. "Maybe fifteen minutes. So we can choose our moment."

"Our moment?" asked Eric. "What moment?"

"Our moment to pounce!" Danny declared. "You see, the Night Scientist will come in and think that the barn is empty. When he least expects it, we jump out. We tie up his hands and feet. I tell him that he'll never get the remote. Never. Every time he tries to catch me, I'll do something like this. I'll outsmart him. So he may as well give up because he's never going to win."

"OK," said Mia, nodding. "But what if he doesn't listen?"

"If he doesn't listen, I'll have to, well, I'll have to get nasty," said Danny.

Mia looked vaguely impressed; Eric looked vaguely anxious.

Danny didn't know what getting nasty would involve, or whether he'd be able to do it, but it felt like that was what he was supposed to say.

In actual fact, he hoped his first plan would work and that the Night Scientist would surrender straightaway.

"Hey, if he doesn't listen, me and Eric can use these," said Mia, pulling a large torch out of her front pocket and a smaller one from her back pocket.

"Woah, you've got two torches?" said Danny.

"Yeah, the one I had last night, plus I pinched Dad's spare," said Mia. "Thought we should be prepared this time."

"Interesting, interesting," said Eric, "but tell you what, why don't you two jump out on him with the torches or whatever. I'll stay hidden. I'll join in if you need me. Kind of like reinforcements."

"No," said Mia. "We're sticking together. We're a team."

She handed Eric the smaller torch. Eric looked at it and took it with a sigh.

"I wish I'd never heard of this bloomin' cosmic remote," he said.

Danny kept recording for another ten minutes. The sun had almost set and the barn was getting darker. There was one bulb hanging near the roof hatch, which threw a narrow shaft of light downwards.

"He'll be here soon," said Mia. "It's dark outside."

"OK," said Danny, and stopped recording. "Let's get ready."

He put the remote on the hay bale and covered it with straw so that it couldn't be seen. He picked up two coils of rope from the floor of the barn and handed them to Mia.

"Now, could you and Eric stand at the far end?" he instructed.

Danny stayed by the remote, ready to press Play as soon as the door was unbolted.

A few minutes went past. The three children waited and waited.

8
POWER OFF

It was pitch black outside.

Danny looked at the time on his remote:

18:58.

18:58 became **18:59**.

The second **18:59** became

19:00, a bolt was slung back.

Danny pressed Play and ran over to join his friends. The image of the barn was projected on top of them. Anyone who walked in would think that the barn was completely empty.

The door shuddered open and the Night Scientist entered. He was followed by six robot parrots, waddling uneasily on their metal claws.

The Night Scientist swivelled his head to the left and right and made a loud growling noise. Then he removed a metal box from his pocket. It was the same metal box that he had used when he broke into Danny's house. He tapped it twice and it started to beep.

"They can't be far," said the Night Scientist. "According to the transmitter, the remote is less than a hundred metres away."

The parrots shuffled from side to side and shook their wings.

"Andre, you go north, Margery, you go west, Petrarch, you go south-west; the rest of you, head for the marshes," ordered the Night Scientist.

The parrots swivelled round, spread their wings and flew out through the barn door.

Behind their invisible barrier, Danny motioned to his friends to stay quiet and still.

The Night Scientist walked forwards and

stood in the dead centre of the barn, about a metre away from where the remote was hidden under a clump of straw.

He looked again at the transmitter and barked angrily. He began to pace backwards and forwards, mumbling to himself. Danny flinched as the Night Scientist slammed his fist down on the hay bale a few centimetres away from the remote's hiding place. One frustrated punch would pulverise it.

The Night Scientist stopped walking and looked up at the roof.

"I thought you'd stay and finish this, boy," he said out loud. 'I didn't think you'd run away again!"

He tapped the transmitter twice.

"Strange, it's not moving," he said. "Maybe one of the birds has caught him."

The Night Scientist rubbed his hands with glee.

"That must be it, the birds have got him," he growled. "What else could it possibly be?"

Then a dark look passed across the Night Scientist's face. He spun round on his heels and stared at the false wall of the barn, where Danny and his friends were hiding. He walked slowly towards it, sniffing the air like a wolf. He was staring directly at Danny now. He seemed to notice the faint shaft of light that was pouring out of the remote and projecting the recorded image on to the barn wall.

"Now!" shouted Danny.

The three friends leapt through the air and knocked the Night Scientist backwards. They had appeared as if from nowhere, flying through the hidden wall.

"Curses!" spluttered the Night Scientist.

In a few seconds he was bound hand and foot. Danny picked up the remote from the floor of the barn and pointed it at him.

"It's over," Danny declared. "You'll never have it! Every time you come for it, something like this will happen. And if you escape, I'll rewind time, and catch you again."

The Night Scientist laughed.

"I'm not joking, I mean it," said Danny.

The Night Scientist laughed again.

"Did you really think this could be settled with words?" he asked.

"What do you mean?" said Danny.

"I realised last time we met that you wouldn't give up the remote without a fight. So a fight is what we're going to have."

Danny tried to speak, but no words came out.

"That's why I brought you here," said the Night Scientist. "This barn didn't exist yesterday. I built it specially for you. Specially for us."

Danny glanced up and around.

"I chose the spot carefully," said the Night Scientist. "It's surrounded by marshland. It's miles from the nearest town. Nobody will interrupt us."

"I – don't – under—" Danny stammered.

"So you have me bound hand and foot," growled the Night Scientist. "Now's your chance. Strike, boy! Strike! Finish me off!"

Danny tried to speak again, but he was mesmerised by the Night Scientist's angry eyes.

"I'll take over, if you like, Danny," said Mia, stepping forwards. She pulled out the torch, twirled it up into her hand and aimed it at the Night Scientist's face.

The Night Scientist shook his head and chuckled. "Not this time, young lady. I'm covered in protective cream. And I'm wearing my blackout jacket. They're no defence against direct sunlight, but they can certainly handle a two-watt torch bulb. Or indeed a thirty-watt light bulb." He pointed up at the light hanging from the roof.

"You're bluffing," said Mia.

The Night Scientist yawned. "You know, it feels as if I'm 'working on my tan'. But heavens above, look at the time! We must get down to business."

He put his teeth over his bottom lip and whistled.

The barn began to creak.

The Night Scientist smiled an eerie smile. Then he whistled again.

A giant hinge seemed to squeak, and a huge crank hissed. The roof of the barn lifted off like a lid. The walls fell outwards and hit the ground with a deafening thump. The three children and the Night Scientist were now sitting underneath the night sky, surrounded by a few bales of hay. They were hit by a blast of wind from the surrounding marshland, which swept most of the hay off the barn floor and out into the countryside beyond.

The Night Scientist shouted: "Parrots, back to base!"

He looked at Danny and Mia and said: "Spring-loaded foundations. Every custom-made mechanical criminal death trap should have them."

"Danny!" cried Eric. "*Please* can we leave now!"

"You should take your friend's advice," said the Night Scientist. "My parrots are about to peck you to pieces."

"Stop him, Danny! Stop him!" Mia urged. "Use your remote to blast him into space or something."

But before Danny had a chance to press his remote, he was distracted by a high-pitched shriek. He looked up and saw six parrots shooting through the air like javelins. His thumb hovered over Rewind and Pause, but all he could think about was running away. The Night Scientist was right. He couldn't stay and fight. He wasn't prepared to hurt the Night Scientist, even though this was the man who had tried to kill his sister, and his best friend, and his Uncle Charlie.

While he tried to work out a plan, he noticed that Eric had already run off into the darkness.

Mia hissed, "Danny, come on," and darted off too.

Danny dashed after his sister, just as three of the parrots whistled past his ear.

Then there was nothing but panting and gasping as the three children ran through the soft mud, trying to keep together in spite of the blackness and the wind and the water everywhere.

"Danny, there's got to be something you can do!" puffed Mia.

Eric tripped over with a wail and Mia helped him up.

"Where are we?" whimpered Eric. "How can we know where we're going when we don't even know where we are!"

They heard the beating of wings overhead, and started to run again.

"I can't believe he built that barn just for tonight," said Mia between gasps. "That's how much he wants the remote!"

"I'm going to Rewind us out of here," said Danny as he ran. "Get us back to town again. Are you ready?"

"At last!" exclaimed Eric.

"You'll forget everything that just happened. Is that OK?" said Danny.

"OK? It's brilliant!" said Eric.

"Oh, don't press Rewind just yet," said a voice from above them.

They all stopped running.

Two of the parrots dropped the Night Scientist gently on to the ground in front of them. He stretched his arms out and gave a little cough.

"Why shouldn't I press Rewind?" asked Danny, in as brave a voice as he could muster.

"Because then our little fight will last for ever and ever," said the Night Scientist, "instead of ending tonight."

He clicked his fingers and a parrot appeared as if from nowhere, snatched the remote from Danny's hand and dropped it at the Night Scientist's feet.

"No!" screamed Danny.

But two other parrots had him by the shoulders and were suspending him a metre above the ground.

"No! No! No! Give it to me! Give it to me!" shouted Danny, kicking and writhing and lashing out and clawing at the air.

The other four parrots had lifted up Eric and Mia.

The Night Scientist picked up the remote with a smile of wild excitement playing across his lips.

"Let's st-start by pr-pressing Pause," he stammered, as if he was almost too scared to touch it.

Danny had shouted himself out and was now a limp rag in the parrots' claws.

The Night Scientist lifted up his thumb and placed it on the Pause button.

"When you're Paused, it will be easier for my friends to peck you into mush," he said.

But still he didn't press Pause. It was like he didn't want the moment to end. His nostrils flared and his cheek twitched.

"I can't believe it, I can't believe it, I can't believe it," he whispered.

He took a deep breath and brought his

thumb down on the Pause button.

The parrots still flapped. The children still panted. The wind still blew.

He pressed Pause again.

Time passed.

He pressed Pause again and again, more urgently and fiercely each time.

"Why isn't it...?" the Night Scientist stammered. "I don't..."

Then his expression changed and he seemed to understand.

"Of course. Very clever, Charles, very clever. Andre!" he barked. "Bring me the boy's thumb."

The parrot that was holding Danny's left shoulder tilted its head to one side.

"His thumb, Andre, his thumb. Just peck it

off!" ordered the Night Scientist.

Danny was dropped on to the ground. He landed like a sack of potatoes and slumped on to his side.

One of the parrots perched on his wrist.

This was too much for Mia. She kicked off her boots, aiming one squarely at the Night Scientist's head. It hit him just above the eyebrow and knocked him on to his back. This seemed to panic the parrots, who dropped her and Eric and flew round in confused circles. The parrot on Danny's wrist hopped across the mud towards its master.

"Danny, get up! Get up!" shouted Mia.

Danny seemed to stir. "My remote," he whispered.

"We don't have time for that," hissed Mia. She could see that the Night Scientist was coming round.

"Come on!" she snapped. "Eric, you too!"

"No! My remote!" bawled Danny.

"This way! Now!" shouted Mia.

She grabbed her brother by the collar and

dragged him across the mud, shooing Eric along with her other hand.

She heard the Night Scientist barking angrily in the darkness and Danny moaning about going back and getting his remote and how this was the end of everything. She realised she would have to take charge, because Danny was too devastated to say or do anything.

The next fifteen minutes were a blur. All Mia could think about was how cold and wet her feet were getting. She hadn't had time to retrieve her boots after kicking them off, so she was squelching through the soft, damp marsh in her socks. Within a few minutes the socks were black and heavy with mud, the ends flopping about and constantly threatening to trip her over. She could feel mud oozing between her toes and seeping under her toenails. For a split second she thought about home and her mother's reaction if she came anywhere near the house looking like this.

She kept tearing forwards, urging the boys on.

A bird shrieked overhead. She didn't think it was one of the parrots, but she couldn't be sure. So she steered the boys away from it.

At last the ground grew firmer. She slowed down very slightly.

Then she heard the Night Scientist's voice. In the darkness, it sounded like he was next to her, whispering in her ear, but she knew her mind was playing tricks with her. He was issuing orders, at least a hundred metres away.

"The footprints are heading north! Fly north!"

Eric seemed to whimper. Mia shushed him.

Out of the corner of her eye, she saw a light.

"This way!" she hissed.

The light grew larger and soon revealed itself to be one end of an old farmhouse. Another two lights flickered on: the headlights of a truck parked outside.

Mia wasn't sure whether to cry out. It could be one of the Night Scientist's friends in the truck, or the Night Scientist himself.

As the children grew closer, Mia watched the

driver climb out of the truck and disappear into the house. However, the headlights were still on and the engine was still running. Mia didn't think twice. Dragging the boys behind her, she sprinted round to the back of the truck.

Perfect, she thought. It was open to the sky, with no roof or sides, loaded up with bales of hay.

"Come on," she whispered.

She got herself on board and pulled Danny and Eric up.

"Cover yourselves," she hissed.

The boys mechanically pulled straw over themselves.

"Heads down," she ordered.

The boys lay flat.

They lay there in the darkness, while the engine rumbled on. Finally the door of the house slammed, then the door of the truck squeaked open and banged shut. They were moving.

After ten minutes, Mia began to breathe more steadily.

"He won't find us now," she whispered.

A split second later there was a rushing noise and the frantic flapping of wings. Instinctively the three children dived deeper under the straw.

The parrot swept over their heads, then banked left, preparing for another attack. It circled twice clockwise, then it seemed to turn round and circle twice anticlockwise. It flew upside down for a couple of seconds. Finally its wings went stiff and it dropped like a stone.

"Look out!" Eric exclaimed.

The parrot landed with a whoomph on one of the hay bales. The truck driver seemed not to hear, because he kept driving.

"Be careful, be careful," said Mia.

But Eric was already inspecting it.

"There's a dent in its head," said Eric. "When you kicked off your boot it must have rebounded off the Night Scientist and hit this parrot. It kept functioning for a while, but now it's finally short circuited."

"You're sure?" asked Mia.

Eric opened a panel in its breast and yanked a tangle of wires out.

"I am now," said Eric.

Mia sat down and breathed a sigh of relief.

"This is so cool," said Eric. "When I get home, I'll rewire it. It will be my new robot. To make up for the one they broke."

"Now hang on—" said Mia.

"I thought this was the worst night of my life, but not any more," added Eric.

Mia was going to argue, but Eric was already poking about inside the parrot's metal ribcage. It was as if he had completely forgotten the past five hours.

"Your friend is a fully paid-up, dyed-in-the-wool, cast-iron supernerd, you know that," she said to Danny.

Danny was lying on his back, staring at the sky, his eyes brimming with tears.

"Come on Danny," said Mia softly. "We're alive."

"He's got it," murmured Danny.

"But he can't use it, didn't you see?" answered Mia. "That's why I had to get you out of there."

"He's won," said Danny.

"He hasn't, not yet," said Mia. "The remote's linked to you in some way. He wanted your hand, your thumb. It's like only your thumb can make it work."

This made Danny think for a few seconds. But then he looked miserable again.

"It's gone," he whispered.

Mia decided to leave her brother alone. They'd talk again later, when the shock of losing his remote had worn off.

They bumped along through the darkness.

The silence was occasionally broken by Danny's tearful murmurs and Eric's growls of concentration as he pored over the parrot's complicated circuitry.

The truck slowed, and stopped.

"Down," whispered Mia.

Eric hid under a hay bale, taking the parrot with him.

The truck driver opened the door and crunched through gravel.

Mia waited till his steps had receded, and then slipped out of the truck. She looked at her surroundings, the driveway of a large house, lit by bright lamps.

"I know this place," she murmured to herself. "Get out, get out!" she shouted at the boys. "It's Buxton Park Hotel. My friend Selina's dad works here. It's only a few miles from home."

Eric leapt out of the truck; Danny crawled out reluctantly.

The night was nearly over. Mia guided them across a series of fields and through a maze of deserted roads. Within an hour they were on the high street.

There was a police car outside Eric's house. Eric knocked on the door and disappeared into his mother's arms.

Mia said to Danny, "I wonder if ours even noticed we were gone."

Danny grunted, still lost in his own thoughts.

Mia got out her front door key. She ushered Danny in before her. The house was the same as ever: silent, lifeless, spotlessly clean.

"Stay in my room tonight," she said to Danny. "It's safer that way."

Mia realised that she wanted to look after Danny now. She had never really enjoyed picking on him, but felt that it was what her parents wanted. She wasn't interested in her parents any more.

"OK," said Danny with a shrug.

So, just as dawn broke, Danny and Mia went to sleep, Danny lying like a starfish on Mia's bed and Mia curled up like a cat on her beanbag. Their dreams were full of killer birds and a man with eyes like a snake and arms reaching out of swamps, pulling them under.

But they slept on, too tired to run any more that night. It was as if their bodies knew they would need all their energy and strength for the following day when the challenges they would face would make the events of yesterday feel like a pleasant childhood memory, something to play over and over again in your head, as if no time had passed between that day and this.

9
HELP

Danny was the first to wake up. He felt for the remote on his chest, panicked, and then remembered.

However he did not wallow in self-pity as he had the day before. A few hours' sleep had worked wonders. Now he was determined to get the remote back.

He swung his legs out of bed and crossed the room. A floorboard squeaked and Mia woke up.

"Danny, what's going on?' she murmured.

"Hi Mia," said Danny, looking guilty.

"What are you up to? Where are you going?" she asked, more fully awake now.

"I'm just, er, going out..." stammered Danny.

Mia clambered up and stood in front of the door, her arms folded. She shook her head.

"You're staying here until I can work out somewhere safer for you to hide out."

"But, Mia, listen..."

"He's coming after you, Danny," said Mia sternly.

"Good!" Danny blurted out.

"He'll send one of his robots and it'll tear your hand off!" cried Mia.

"I need it back, Mia, I need it back!" shouted Danny. "I can't – I can't – face – life without it."

There was a knock on the door and Mr and Mrs Danger appeared.

"For heaven's sake," their mother huffed. "What's all this noise?"

"Noise," said their father, wagging his finger slowly.

"And you were both so good yesterday," added their mother. "We hardly heard a peep out of you."

"Peep," said their father, nodding in agreement.

"And since *when* were you allowed to play in your sister's room?" said his mother, looking at Danny.

"Mmm," said Danny. Out of habit, he was reaching for his remote, preparing to rewind the whole conversation.

"Back to your room!" screeched their mother.

"It's OK, Mum, I asked him in," said Mia softly.

It was as if their mother had been slapped round the face with a wet flannel. She froze and stared at the opposite wall.

"Muriel?" said their father.

"Mmm?" asked their mother blankly. She seemed to realise where she was and blinked twice.

"What did you say, Mia?" she asked.

"I said I invited Danny in," said Mia. "He's going to clean my windows and then he's going to polish my wardrobe," she added.

"Oh, oh, I see," said their mother. "Well, if you think he'll do an acceptable job. Which I very much doubt."

"He's no good," said their father, "and never has been."

"When you're done here," said their mother to Danny, "you'll help your father unblock the drains."

The bedroom door was closed.

"This is *exactly* why I need my remote," said Danny.

"Danny, at least you're alive," said Mia. "If the Night Scientist gets you..."

There was another knock on the bedroom door. Danny and Mia looked at each other quizzically. The door opened and they saw Jasper and Roxie, the two young people who had been beamed out of Danny's remote the day before. Roxie's hair was green today and Jasper had even bigger headphones round his neck.

"Hey Danny," said Roxie. "We've been waiting in your room all morning."

"Bit bare in there, mate," said Jasper. "A poster or two wouldn't go amiss."

"As you know, Danny," said Roxie, "the Night Scientist has got the remote. Your uncle told us that, if this ever happened, we should come and get you."

"My – my uncle?" asked Danny hesitantly. "You spoke to my uncle? He's OK?"

Jasper and Roxie looked at each other.

"Hey, do you want to listen to an actual conversation between two Martians?" asked Jasper, holding out his headphones.

"Stop it, Jasper," said Roxie. "You'd want to know the truth if it was *your* uncle."

"Depends on the uncle," said Jasper. "If it was Smelly Uncle Trevor, I wouldn't give a monkey's."

"The thing is, Danny," said Roxie, putting her arm on Danny's shoulder. "We're not sure. He set off to find you two days ago."

Danny looked down at the floor.

"All I can say is, your uncle's gone missing before," said Roxie.

"Like about a million times," said Jasper.

"And he always comes back," said Roxie.

"Sorry," said Mia, stepping forwards. "Who are you? You could be anyone."

"Hey, you must be Mia," said Roxie. "Let's bump fists. Charlie said you'd come through for your brother."

Roxie held out a clenched fist. Mia touched it warily with her own.

"Look, sister," said Roxie, "I wish we had time to explain, but we don't. Jasper will leave you with a booklet about EUREKA!"

Jasper patted his pockets and murmured: "Left it in the car."

He opened the palm of his hand and frowned at it as hard as he could. A booklet slowly materialised, one particle at a time.

"Eat after reading," said Jasper, handing it to Mia with a wink.

"Now we have to get Danny to the Professor," said Roxie, flicking a chunk of green hair over her shoulder. She crouched down and put a hand on Danny's shoulder. "Do you need to say goodbye to anyone? Friends? Relatives?"

"Just Mia and Eric," said Danny.

Mia was skimming the booklet about EUREKA! "I can't believe Uncle Charlie is part of this," said Mia. "EUREKA! is amazing, Danny. They've only got seven agents, but they protect the whole world from people like the Night Scientist."

"OK, cool," said Danny. "So – so – I should go with them, should I?"

"Definitely," said Mia. "Sounds like they save the planet twice a week and no one even notices."

Mia turned to Danny and gave him a hug, holding him tight for a full minute.

"I'm going to say goodbye to Eric too," said Danny.

Mia nodded.

"Do you need me to get Mum and Dad out of the way?" she asked Jasper and Roxie.

"No, it's OK," said Roxie. "Jasper hypnotised them. They now think they're warthogs. We thought it was easiest."

So Mia stood by the front door, waving Danny off, while her mother rooted through the cupboards for food and her father dug up the front garden with his bare hands.

Danny knocked on Eric's front door. Jasper and Roxie waited in the street.

Eric opened the door with the robot parrot under his arm.

"I've got it working, Danny," he said excitedly. "Properly this time. Not like my robot. It can go left, go right. It hardly ever flies into things."

"Cool," said Danny. "Hey, sorry if I got you in trouble last night."

"It's fine," said Eric. "I just told my mum I got on the wrong bus home from the shops. She's happy enough now."

"Erm, there's something else," said Danny. "I've got to go away. You remember Jasper and Roxie – "

"The holograms? From your remote?" asked Eric.

"I'm going away with them," said Danny.

"For quite a long while, I think."

"Oh," said Eric.

Danny nodded mutely.

"Oh," said Eric again.

"Can you look after my books and clothes and everything?" said Danny.

"Of course. They can just stay in the playroom," said Eric.

Then Eric cleared his throat and held out the parrot. "Here," he said.

"What?" replied Danny. "Oh, no, Eric, no, seriously."

"Take it," said Eric. "You're going to need it if you come up against that Night Scientist guy again."

"No, honestly, Eric," said Danny. "I'm sure Jasper and Roxie will look after me."

"Maybe, maybe not," said Eric. "But this parrot definitely will. Look, I think I can build another one myself. The wiring's much easier than I thought."

"But you need to protect yourself too..." said Danny.

"Take it, Danny," said Eric, wedging it under Danny's arm. "Take it."

Danny smiled at his friend. "OK."

"It's all voice activated," said Eric enthusiastically. "Just speak clearly: 'take off', 'fly north', 'fly south'. To switch it on, twist its beak forty-five degrees clockwise. The only thing you must never do is remove this screw here. I put it there to disable its homing instinct."

"Its homing instinct?" asked Danny.

"Yes, it's designed to return to the Night Scientist at the end of every mission," said Eric. "If you take that screw out, that's where it will go. Back to its master."

"Crikey," said Danny, looking warily into the parrot's jewelled eyes.

There was a hoot behind them. Danny turned round and saw Jasper and Roxie in a large white van. It had aerial masts and satellite dishes attached to its roof. Roxie climbed out and slid open the side door.

"Let's roll!" she shouted.

"Wow! Are they making a TV show? Looks like an outside broadcast van!" exclaimed Eric.

He turned to Danny. "When you come back, ask them if I can be on telly. You know, just in the background. Doing a wheelie on my bike or something."

Danny smiled and walked over to the van.

"You'll be in the back with me," said Roxie. "You can put your fluffy toy in the front if you want."

Danny was going to explain that the parrot wasn't a toy, but in the end he just said, "No, he's staying with me."

Danny stepped into the back of the van. It had no windows, but instead it was full of computer terminals, TV screens, humming metal boxes and panels covered in switches and buttons. Roxie slid the door shut, shouted "Go!" and Jasper pulled away. Danny's eyes moved from one monitor to the next. "What is all this stuff?" he said. Roxie smiled.

"The basic tools of a EUREKA! agent," she said. "Your uncle told you about EUREKA!, right?"

"A bit," said Danny. "You go round the world, collecting people's inventions. Or something."

"Sort of," said Roxie. "EUREKA! stands for Experts in Unusual and Remarkable Electro-Kinetic Artefacts."

"Electric Septic What?"

"Magical gadgets. We make sure the bad guys don't get their hands on them."

She pointed to a yellow box with a bleeping radar screen.

"That's BARF. The Brain Activity Reader and Finder. It tells us whenever anyone in the world invents something. See all those red dots. Those are all the people with highly active brains. When the dot goes green, they've finished an invention. So we send an agent to check it out."

She jerked her thumb at a large monitor with a map of the world on it.

"That's PLOP. The Physical Location of Operatives Panel. Shows the whereabouts of all seven EUREKA! agents. We work out which agent is closest to the new invention. Then off they go. Look, that's us there."

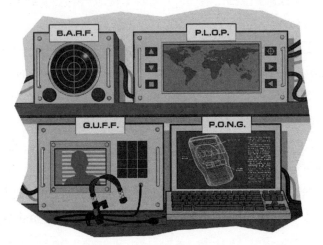

She pointed at a white flashing dot in the south-east of England.

"So, ah, which one's Uncle Charlie?" stammered Danny.

"Like we said, he's, er, gone undercover, so we can't, ah, see him on this map," said Roxie. "I'll just finish the tour. That's GUFF. A video phone that lets us talk to other agents. That's PONG. An online record of every gadget we know about."

"And what's that?" asked Danny, pointing to a square box with a black dial on the front.

"That's the toaster," said Roxie with a smile. "Fancy a slice?"

Danny grinned and shook his head. He decided he liked being with Roxie and Jasper.

Jasper went over a bump and Danny remembered something.

"Can these computers tell you where my remote is?" he asked.

Roxie looked at Danny and shook her head.

"Aren't you going to find it then?" asked Danny.

"Hope so," said Roxie. "Unless the Night Scientist destroys it first."

"*Destroys* it?" exclaimed Danny. "Why would he destroy it?"

"Out of frustration maybe?" said Roxie. "Or spite? Because it won't work for him."

Danny suddenly remembered what Mia had said. "Is that because I'm the only person who can use it?" he asked.

Roxie nodded. "You got it. Charlie made sure it was fingerprint-protected. If anyone else pushes those buttons, it locks 'em out."

Danny wondered how Uncle Charlie had managed to get his fingerprints. Then he remembered his uncle's visit before last when they had played at being detectives. Charlie had rolled Danny's fingers on a large ink block.

So they hadn't been playing after all.

At that moment, Roxie frowned and pulled a catapult out of her back pocket. It had a red handle and yellow elastic and seemed to be buzzing.

"That's weird. It only shakes when there's something hostile in the area," she said.

She banged the metal panel that led to the

driver's cabin. "Jasper, open up the back."

Two seconds later the double doors at the back of the van swung open. They were on an empty country road that whizzed away behind them.

"Hmm," said Roxie. She pressed a button on the handle of her catapult and a small glass sighting disc appeared on top of the right-hand prong. She squinted down it. "Think it's one of the Night Scientist's surveillance droids," said Roxie. "Take a look."

Danny leaned across and saw, in the middle of the sights, a small metal flying fox with black slits for eyes, hovering in front of a cloud.

"OK, Dan, stand back," said Roxie. She pulled a gold pellet out of her front pocket and placed it in the middle of the sling. She stared down the sights again and stretched the sling back as far as it could go. Danny could just about make out the flying fox in the sky: a tiny black dot, at least two miles above the ground. Roxie released the sling, there was a fizzling noise and the black dot instantly vanished, leaving behind a puff of smoke.

"Got a range of five miles," she said. "Fires pellets at a thousand metres per second. Comes in handy in situations like that."

She returned the catapult to her back pocket and closed the back doors of the van.

"Trouble is, that means the Night Scientist knows where we are," said Roxie. "We need to get to the hideout fast."

She was about to tell Jasper to get a move on, when the van screeched to a halt, and they were thrown forwards.

As they were picking themselves up, Jasper slid open the hatch and poked his head through. "Come and look and this," he said.

Roxie climbed out of the side door, followed by Danny clutching his parrot. They joined Jasper in front of the van.

"Hang on," said Roxie. "This is Bardley Park. There's the row of oak trees. So where's the hideout?"

"Exactly," said Jasper. "It's like the ground just swallowed it up."

Danny looked at the large green field and said, "You mean, there used to be a house here?"

Roxie pulled her catapult out of her pocket. It was buzzing loudly.

Jasper turned to Roxie and said, "Are you thinking tunnelling animals? The Night Scientist attacked the foundations?"

Roxie looked at her catapult and said, "I'm thinking we've got to get out of here. Now."

They all climbed into the front and sat side by side. Before Jasper could turn the key in the ignition, the van lurched backwards and the back wheels seemed to drop half a metre into the ground.

"Something's underneath us," said Roxie. "Drive, Jasper, drive!"

The van lurched forwards and its front wheels sank into the road. The windscreen was now level with the tarmac.

"We're sinking too fast, we can't move!" Jasper yelled.

As they disappeared further into the ground,

a large black metal beetle scuttled up the bonnet and stared at them through the windscreen. It had sharp metal pincers on its head.

Danny instinctively reached for his remote. He checked his left pocket and his right, before he remembered.

"Beetles! I should have known!" exclaimed Roxie. "They must have dragged the house underground too."

Two more beetles climbed on to the windscreen and tapped it angrily with their pincers.

"We've got to get out of here, Rox!" said Jasper.

"You don't say," said Roxie. "Come on, up on the roof."

Jasper wound down his window and swung himself on to the roof of the van. He put his arms back into the cabin and shouted, "Come on, Danny."

Danny looked down at the parrot in his lap.

"Take this first," he said, holding it out.

So the parrot and then Danny and then Roxie were pulled out of the van and on to the roof.

Danny looked over the edge of the van and saw, about a metre down, dozens of beetles scurrying around the wheels and scratching at the doors.

Again, he fumbled in his pocket, searching for his remote. Again, he stopped when he remembered.

"Can you lift us out?" Roxie said to Jasper.

"I don't know," said Jasper. "The heaviest thing I've ever lifted was, you know, that sofa bed."

The van tilted further back. Danny managed to keep his balance by using his parrot as a crutch.

"Come on, Jasper," whispered Roxie. "Let's fly through the sky."

"OK, OK," said Jasper. "I'll try."

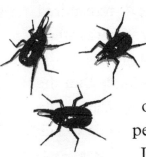

He closed his eyes and frowned. Roxie pulled her catapult out of her back pocket and moved to the front of the roof, firing pellet after pellet at the insects below.

Jasper was holding his hands out. Danny felt the van jerk forwards and then move, very slightly, upwards.

"That's it, Jasper! That's it!" shouted Roxie, blasting another beetle to bits with her catapult.

Jasper's body started to shake as the van moved another half a metre out of the hole. Danny looked over the edge of the roof again and saw hundreds more beetles pouring on to the road.

Then he looked at the parrot under his arm and seemed to remember something. He twisted its beak round forty-five degrees clockwise and said: "Fight the beetles!"

The parrot's eyes lit up and it hopped off the edge of the van, dropping into the hole and attacking any beetle it saw.

"Can't do – much – more," murmured Jasper as the van rose higher. His face was white and his jaw was slack.

Danny watched as his parrot landed on the road ahead with three beetles in its claws. The parrot jabbed its beak into each beetle's neck and pulled out a crackling tangle of wires.

While he was watching this, Danny didn't notice a beetle sprinting up the windscreen and scuttling across the roof. The beetle stopped and looked at Danny's hand. It opened its pincers and closed them around Danny's thumb.

Danny screamed.

At the same moment, Roxie cut the beetle in two with a well-aimed pellet.

Danny looked down at the two dots of blood at the base of his thumb.

"He was a sneaky one, wasn't he?" said Roxie, turning back round and firing more pellets at the beetles in the road.

As Jasper lifted the van another metre into the air, Danny could see the hole beneath them more clearly. It was nothing but a writhing mass of black metal shapes, thousands and thousands of beetles.

Danny wanted his remote. He needed his remote. He felt useless without it. He felt pointless.

Jasper let out a massive groan and slumped forwards. The van dropped back towards the ground and Roxie and Danny nearly fell off the sides. The van landed awkwardly, its front wheels hit the road, its back wheels were still hanging over the edge of the hole.

"I'm sorry," Jasper was murmuring. "I'm sorry."

Roxie was still firing her catapult at the beetles. She looked over her shoulder at Danny. "You need to get out of here! How strong is your parrot? Can it carry you?"

Danny nodded.

"Then go! Now! We'll find you!"

Danny shouted, "Parrot! Return to base!" It appeared by his side a split second later. It had a beetle's leg sticking out of its beak.

Danny said: "Pick me up and fly west."

He was pulled off the roof of the van and into the sky.

As they soared above the road, Danny watched the van tilt further back into the hole. Jasper had come round and was standing next to Roxie. The hole, the road and the fields around it were covered with black shapes.

Danny realised that he had made an important decision. He reached up with his hand until he felt the screw that was sticking out of the parrot's neck. This was the screw that Eric had inserted to disable the parrot's homing instinct. If Danny removed the screw, the parrot would return to the Night Scientist.

Danny removed the screw.

The parrot veered round and flew east. It seemed to flap its wings with fresh urgency and purpose. Danny put the screw in his pocket and imagined that the remote was back in his hand, the amber crystal glowing gently in his palm.

"The remote will make everything right again," whispered Danny into the wind.

10
POWER ON

They flew over forests and fields and they flew over towns and cities. The land suddenly ran out and they were flying over the sea, with nothing but water stretching out on all sides. The wind picked up, buffeting them and spraying them with sea water. As the parrot flew higher, the temperature dropped, and Danny's teeth started to chatter.

As they flew higher, Danny stopped thinking about anything except how cold he was. First he lost sensation in his fingers, then his toes, then his ears, then his nose, then his lips turned blue and his cheeks turned purple and finally he went stiff as a board and couldn't move anything except his eyes.

He was about to pass out when the parrot veered sharply to the left and he was hit by a warm current of air. Suddenly, he could move his arms and legs again. Danny breathed a deep sigh of relief. A few seconds later they were flying over land again, clipping the tops of pine trees and mountain ferns. For a while, they flew beside a flock of blackbirds, who looked warily at the parrot and cheeped quietly amongst themselves.

The blackbirds dropped away and the parrot began to slow down. His eyes seemed to be focusing on someone or something just over the horizon. A few seconds later the trees and hills vanished, and they were flying across a small flat clearing. In the middle of the clearing, there was a series of buildings: houses, huts, factories, warehouses and cabins. Danny noticed that, from above, they spelled out a word:

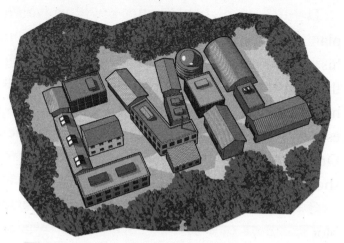

This wasn't a good sign.

But then again, he had clearly reached his destination. Danny was sure that the cosmic remote would be here.

The parrot flew towards a long brick building in the middle of the complex. Danny wasn't ready to meet the Night Scientist yet, so he prised the parrot's claws off his sweater, checked that there were bushes and trees to break his fall, and then dropped quickly to the ground.

He clambered out of a clump of ferns and looked at the two small huts in front of him.

He thought that he'd better come up with a plan. He decided to start with the buildings on his left and sneak into them one by one, going through every box and drawer and cupboard till he had found his remote. If he saw anyone – especially the Night Scientist – he would hide. Only when he had his remote back would he show himself openly.

The first building was a long white concrete block with two storeys and tinted windows that prevented Danny from seeing inside. From above, it would have formed the bottom of the E in EVIL.

The door was ajar and Danny slipped inside. He found himself in a corridor with a door at each end. The door on the left was clearly some kind of fire escape. As Danny got nearer to the door on the right, he began to hear squeaking and whirring and tapping noises. He opened the door quietly.

He found himself in some kind of animal laboratory. There were narrow wooden tables stretching the length of the room. On each table, there were glass cages containing different species of animal. However these weren't ordinary animals; they were the Night Scientist's electronic pets. Danny walked past robot rats and remote-controlled raccoons and mechanical monkeys. Most of them were switched off but occasionally he passed a weasel or a goat that fixed him with a steady glittering eye.

At the end of one of the tables, there was a dog in pieces. It was similar to the dog that had attacked him in the park two short days ago. Its legs had been unscrewed and two springs were sticking out of its eye sockets.

The laboratory was certainly creepy, but in one way it put Danny's mind at rest. He knew for certain that he was in the right place: this was definitely the Night Scientist's lair.

He checked in every cupboard and cabinet for his cosmic remote and then went upstairs. There was nothing there but empty offices.

He moved into the next building. This was a single-storey warehouse containing more animals. However, where the last building had been full of mammals, this one was full of birds. Unlike the mammals in their cages, the birds were hanging from long metal racks that ran parallel to each other. The birds were grouped by species: there was a row of eagles, and then a dozen vultures, and then an albatross or two. They all hung there silently, ready to take off when their master called.

In the next building Danny saw the electronic fish. Robot crabs and eels and octopuses sat in large tanks filled with strange silvery liquid.

The building next to this contained six robot crocodiles. They had collars round their necks and they were all chained to a stake in the middle of the room. They were all switched off except one who opened his mouth wide and snapped it shut as Danny crept past.

So far, there was no sign of the remote.

There was a stretch of straggly yellow grass and then another building. This was tall and narrow like a lighthouse.

Danny darted inside and found himself in a single circular room with a high vaulted ceiling. All along the curved brick walls, somebody had pinned up hundreds of drawings, diagrams, blueprints and maps. Stacks of paper were piled up in the middle of the room. Pens, rulers, protractors and compasses were strewn across the floor. Danny picked up a sheet of paper at random and saw a sketch of what looked like a robot. It looked roughly the same size and shape as a human. He wondered if this was what the Night Scientist was working on now: robot humans as well as robot animals.

Danny kicked through some of the paper on the floor and quickly decided that his remote wasn't here. He was about to leave the building when he saw something glinting next to the door. It looked like the top half of a robot.

Danny was curious and walked towards it. It looked like the Night Scientist had started building one of his robot humans. Danny took another few steps forwards. It was the torso and head of an electronic boy. It had no arms and no legs and its chest was a half-built circuit board.

Danny leaned forwards and squinted at its face. He quickly recoiled. For a few seconds he found it hard to breathe. It was obvious that the robot boy was meant to be an exact replica of himself. He looked at the hair, the nose, the shape of its face. Was the Night Scientist  planning to get rid of him, and replace him with this robot version?

Danny ran out of the building, leaning against the closed door, trying to get his breath back.

He didn't have time to think about what he had just seen. He needed to focus on his remote.

The next building was a small brick hut surrounded by barbed wire, a wire fence and a ditch full of fizzing blue sludge that looked highly toxic. There were signs tied to the wire fence and hammered into the ground behind the ditch.

Danny started looking for ways across the ditch or holes in the fence. There had to be a way in somewhere.

After circling the building three times, he noticed a wooden sign that was outside the barbed wire and the fence. It was leaning to one side and had the word SCRAM painted in the middle of it.

Danny nudged it with his shoulder. It was definitely loose. He shoved it hard and it fell over backwards, sending a sprinkling of soil into the air.

Danny pulled the stake off the back of the sign, twisting it until all the nails came loose. He ran towards the barbed wire, waving the stake in the air. Now he'd be able to get in.

He used the stake to pull the barbed wire up into the air while he crawled under it. Then he used the pointy end of the stake to dig a hole underneath the fence. It took him at least half an hour to make the hole deep enough.

As he was digging, he became more and more convinced that the remote would be in this building. His hands began to shake and he stopped digging for a few seconds. He looked at his right thumb and wiggled it back and forth. He was lucky that it was still there, lucky that it hadn't been snipped off.

When the hole was big enough, Danny slipped under the fence, dragging the stake with him. Now there was nothing between him and the building but the ditch full of strange blue gunk.

He grabbed a handful of grass and threw it into the ditch. Before it had even touched the surface of the blue liquid, it sizzled and vanished into thin air.

Probably best not to swim across, Danny thought to himself.

Instead he glanced down at the stake and smiled. He looked at the other side of the ditch and smiled. He ran at the ditch as fast as he could, planted the stake into the ground and used it like a pole vault to fling himself across the blue channel. He hurtled through the air and landed with a crunch on the grass in front of the building. The stake dropped into the blue sludge and disintegrated into splinters.

Danny clambered to his feet and looked back at the barbed wire and the fence and the ditch. He smiled a relieved smile.

He turned round and looked up at the building. It was about four metres wide and four metres long, not much bigger than a shed or a garage. There were no windows, just a single metal door on the right-hand side.

Danny walked towards this door and turned the handle. It opened with a rusty creak.

Danny stepped inside and closed the door behind him. He looked up and nearly passed out.

The room was dark and bare except for a

marble pedestal right in the centre. On top of the pedestal, Danny saw his cosmic remote. It was lit up by a spotlight that hung from the middle of the ceiling.

Danny stared at his remote without moving for at least two minutes. Then he began to move cautiously towards it. Every step he took, he expected an alarm to go off or a red light to start flashing. But now he was halfway across the room and nothing had happened.

He couldn't believe he was so close to getting his remote back. He couldn't believe that the agony would soon be over.

He took another step forwards. Still, nothing happened.

He ran out of patience and dashed towards his remote, his arms flailing. He grabbed the remote with his right hand. He was so excited, he missed it. So he reached out for it again. Once more, it seemed to slip from his grasp. So he moved his hand towards the remote very slowly, curling his fingers around the sides. He squeezed the remote, expecting to feel its plastic case, its rubber buttons and the crystal on its back. But he felt nothing.

It was then that he realised that the remote wasn't there. It was just a recording.

His heart sank and he felt sick. Then something hissed underneath him and the ground gave way. He was falling.

He threw his arms out but there was nothing to hold on to. He was in a dark chute, falling faster and faster.

He landed on something soft and leapt up straightaway. The momentum of the fall carried him forwards and he did a head over heels, hitting his head on his knee. Everything went black.

11
EJECT

When Danny came round, he wasn't sure where he was or how much time had passed. Just as he had decided to stand up and find out, he heard a whirring noise.

The ground had given way again and now he was on a gigantic slide. He tried slowing down by clamping his hands and feet on to the sides, but it was no use. It was too steep and too slippery.

The slide ran out and he rolled forwards on to a hard grey concrete floor.

He looked up and saw the Night Scientist in front of him.

They were in a massive underground warehouse, lit by ultraviolet panels that were screwed into the walls. There were huge double doors at each end. In the middle of the warehouse there were four or five tables, piled up with computers, circuit boards, screwdrivers, blowtorches, iron rods and gigantic crystals.

"Good evening, Daniel," said the Night Scientist. "And may I be the first to bid you welcome to my humble abode."

Danny stood up and looked at the Night Scientist with what he hoped was a brave face.

"You'll notice the ultraviolet light," said the Night Scientist. "You remember that my skin is ever so slightly sensitive. Then there's the underground location. That's so I can work by day as well as by night. Undisturbed."

"Wh-what do you want with me?" Danny managed to blurt out.

"Don't you want the tour first?" asked the Night Scientist. "Well, if you insist, we can get down to business." He reached into his pocket.

"Here's your remote back."

He threw Danny's remote on to the ground, where it landed with a clatter.

Danny looked at it for a second, then threw himself on to the floor and picked it up.

"I don't get it," said Danny when he was back on his feet. "Last thing I knew, you were trying to cut my thumb off. Have you broken the remote or something? You have, haven't you? You've broken it!"

Danny went to press the Pause button.

"NO!" roared the Night Scientist. Danny froze in terror.

"Excuse my rudeness," continued the Night Scientist in a quieter voice. "Allow me to explain and then you'll be free to use your remote howsoever you choose."

Danny was still too frightened to move, but he managed to nod mutely.

"Your remote fell into my hands yesterday. Initially I tried to get it to work without fingerprint recognition. This I couldn't manage. So early this morning, I took a closer look at the amber crystal in its back. Why, I asked myself, does it need to be so large? Would the remote still work if I split it in two? It turns out, it works just fine. It's funny, you'd have thought that those clever people at EUREKA! would have worked this out. But then, they were probably too busy 'doing good' or 'saving the world' or something equally pathetic."

"I don't understand," stammered Danny.

"What I'm saying is that I don't need your remote," said the Night Scientist, pulling a black baton out of his pocket. "What I'm saying is that I have a better one."

"What?" said Danny, blinking hard.

"I used the half-crystal I took out of your remote to make another remote. I finished it while you were upstairs having a little snooze. Obviously I added a few features of my own. A Brightness button. An Eject button. Makes it a bit more fun."

"So, so why—?" began Danny.

"Why have I given yours back?" said the Night Scientist. "Just my strange sense of humour, I suppose. You see, I intend to Rewind time. I thought you might like to stop me."

"I don't see what you—" murmured Danny.

"Then I might Pause time for a while," continued the Night Scientist. "Maybe rob a few banks. Settle a few scores. Your uncle and your sister might not feel so good when I've finished. After that, I might press Fast Forward and see how you react to the news."

He pointed the remote at Danny. "Goodbye," he said.

Danny instinctively pointed his remote at the Night Scientist.

"Good," said the Night Scientist with a smile.

Danny saw the Night Scientist's finger pushing a button. He began to feel the strangest sensation, as if someone was tugging both of his arms, as if part of his brain was being slowly wiped clean and the warehouse in front of him was losing its outlines and becoming one big grey blob.

He guessed that time was being rewound. He

tried to move his thumb but it felt impossible, like it was encased in concrete. He fought harder, willing his thumb towards the Fast Forward button, determined to cancel out what the Night Scientist was doing, growling with frustration when his thumb moved backwards not forwards.

Something gave way and his thumb was wedged down on Fast Forward. Time seemed to stop. He saw the Night Scientist in front of him, looking annoyed. Then everything tumbled forwards, he felt a huge pressure lift from his shoulders, and the warehouse came back into focus. He let go of Fast Forward.

"Very good," snarled the Night Scientist. "I pressed Rewind. You pressed Fast Forward. We cancelled each other out. But what next?"

Danny saw the Night Scientist pressing another button. It was as if someone had poured ice into his veins. The warehouse was still in front of him, but he felt separate from it, like he was a cut-out or a waxwork. The Night Scientist must have pressed Pause. Danny tried his hardest to press the Play button. His thumb moved feebly like he was an invalid. But somehow he pressed Play and his body felt warm and alive again, he smelled the stale air of the warehouse and he felt the hard concrete floor under his shoes.

"Mnnrrgh," growled the Night Scientist. "I wasn't expecting our duel to last this long. Well, this should finish it."

But Danny had already pressed Rewind. The Night Scientist gasped and forced his thumb on to Fast Forward. Then Danny pressed Pause, but the Night Scientist had already pressed Play. Danny tried pressing Fast Forward, hoping that this would catch the Night Scientist off guard. But the Night Scientist calmly wedged his thumb on to the Rewind button.

Both Danny and the Night Scientist lowered their remotes for a few seconds, breathing heavily.

"Enough!" said the Night Scientist. "It's time to end this. I'm going to press Eject now. When I point it at someone, they get wiped off the face of the earth. Ready?"

Danny was about to press Rewind again, when he saw a beam of light shoot out of the end of the Night Scientist's remote. He leapt out of the way. The Night Scientist pointed his remote at Danny again. Another lightning bolt shot out of the end. Danny rolled over backwards.

"Now this *is* fun," declared the Night Scientist.

Danny began to realise that there was no way of winning.

He was about to throw his remote at the Night Scientist's head when he saw its Play button flashing. He frowned at it for a second or two.

Another jolt of light leapt across the room. Danny sprang forwards, glancing back at the smoking black crater that had appeared in the ground.

As soon as he felt steady on his feet, he pressed Play.

He heard Uncle Charlie's voice whispering: "Buy us some time, Dan. We'll do the rest." Then there was a crackle and silence.

For three seconds Danny stood absolutely still. This must mean that Uncle Charlie was alive and well and very close by.

Danny tried not to grin; he tried not to giggle. He needed to act quickly.

"Wait!" he called out.

The Night Scientist was aiming the remote at Danny's chest. "Ah, I don't think so," he said.

"Look, you've won, you've won," said Danny. "But before you press Eject, just tell me what happened to my uncle."

The Night Scientist flicked the remote up and pressed it against his mouth.

"Hmm," he said. "I owe you that much, I suppose. Lay your remote down in front of you."

Danny put his remote on the ground.

"Well, you see, it was quite brilliant," said the Night Scientist, gazing at the far wall. "Even if I do say so myself. Your uncle never really stood a chance."

At that moment, Danny noticed something happening over the Night Scientist's shoulder. A column of light had appeared in the far right-hand corner of the warehouse.

"That's the trouble with *good people*," said the Night Scientist. "They make it too easy. They don't really *challenge* you."

The column of light now had hard edges and definite colours.

"But I digress," said the Night Scientist. "So anyway, I found your uncle in a small hut on the banks of the River Niger. He was disguised as a humble fisherwoman, but he didn't fool me for a second."

The column of light was now clearly a human being. The outline sharpened further and revealed Uncle Charlie holding a shoe in his right hand. Danny forced himself to look at the floor.

"I released one of my giant fish into the river—" said the Night Scientist.

The shoe whizzed through the air and hit the Night Scientist on the back of the head. The remote flew out of his hand.

"Grab it, Danny!" shouted Uncle Charlie.

Danny had already leapt forwards. He stuffed the Night Scientist's remote into his pocket.

"Blast it all!" yelled the Night Scientist as he lay sprawled on the floor.

Uncle Charlie scooped Danny up in his arms and said, "Got you, mate. Sorry for the delay."

Danny held tightly to Uncle Charlie and said, "I wasn't even sure if you were alive or dead!"

"I know," said Uncle Charlie. "Sorry about that. And sorry for not telling you everything right at the start. But listen, we'll talk later – we've got to make sure that – hey, where's he gone?"

The Night Scientist was no longer on the

ground in front of them.

"What a touching scene. Uncle and nephew reunited," said a voice behind them. They swung round and saw the Night Scientist standing on his workbench. "Such a shame I have to break it up."

Danny held his remote out and placed his thumb over the Pause button.

"Remotes! Return to owner!" cried the Night Scientist.

Danny felt his remote being sucked out of his hand. At the same time, the Night Scientist's remote slipped out of Danny's pocket and zipped through the air. The Night Scientist caught them both.

"Did you honestly think I'd give you a fully working remote? Without any kind of homing device?" said the Night Scientist.

He pointed one remote at Danny and one at Uncle Charlie.

"Time to finish this," he growled.

"Now, hang on, Herbert," said Uncle Charlie. "I didn't come here to fight. Think about it. Why do you think I hit you with a shoe?"

"Yes, what is it with you people and footwear?" growled the Night Scientist, rubbing the back of his head.

"Danny's sister showed me how to aim," said Uncle Charlie.

"You've seen Mia!" whispered Danny.

"Shh," said Uncle Charlie. He looked up at the Night Scientist. "I wanted to knock you for six, but not seriously hurt you. Because I'm here in my official capacity as Vice-President of EUREKA! We want you to join us."

The Night Scientist chuckled and put his finger on the Eject button. "You must take me for a fool. You know I'd never join your dismal organisation."

"Dismal, eh?" said Uncle Charlie. "So how do you think I got in here? I'll tell you. Direct matter transfer. It's the ability to move objects through space with the mind alone. And have you heard of a domino pill? Swallow it and you can do any sum, any equation, any calculation.

What about an earth cruiser? You can get to the equator in three minutes."

The Night Scientist seemed to be thinking. "You're lying," he said finally. "You'd never let me near any of those devices."

"Black-hole corks. Planet shifters. Sun shoes – you too can walk on the surface of the sun."

"Those things can't possibly exist," said the Night Scientist with a sneer.

At that moment there was a deafening bang. It came from behind the huge metal doors that stood at the far end of the warehouse.

Uncle Charlie smiled and glanced at his watch. "Right on time," he said.

There was a second ear-splitting bang. This time a huge dent appeared in one of the metal doors.

"Intruders!" exclaimed the Night Scientist. He spun round and pointed his remote at the door, keeping Danny's remote trained on Uncle Charlie.

There was a third bang, the loudest so far, that shook the ground and hammered the walls.

The dent in the door was gigantic now.

"What's going on?" whispered Danny.

"The cavalry's arrived," whispered back Uncle Charlie.

"My robot army should have detected this," growled the Night Scientist, placing his thumb on the Pause button of his remote.

However, before he could press it, the metal doors were smashed open and there, sitting on the back of a robot rhino, was Eric. Beside him, sitting on a robot horse, was Mia. Behind them there was a wall of robot animals: monkeys, crocodiles, dogs, crows, lizards and mice.

"What is the meaning of this?" spluttered the Night Scientist, his yellow eyes flashing.

"Get ready," whispered Uncle Charlie. "When I say *now*, push the workbench over."

"Oh. Oh, OK," stammered Danny, still looking at Eric and Mia in astonishment.

"Robot army! Stand down!" exclaimed the Night Scientist. He seemed to have forgotten about the remotes; he held them loosely at his sides.

"Robot army! About turn!" shouted the Night Scientist.

"Robot army!" yelled Eric. "Attack!"

"Now!" shouted Uncle Charlie.

Uncle Charlie and Danny dashed forwards and heaved over the workbench, sending the Night Scientist flying. The remotes spiralled through the air. At the same time, all of the robot animals tore across the warehouse. The birds flew like arrows; the mice sped like bullets; the lizards hurtled like rockets. Eric's rhino and Mia's horse put their heavy metal heads between their front legs and charged.

"No!" shouted the Night Scientist. "Destroy! Mutilate! Kill!"

Two of the dogs picked up the remotes and retreated. The crocodile picked up the Night Scientist in his steel jaws and tossed him to the seal, who balanced him on his nose before butting him towards the zebra.

"Zebra to moose," called out Eric. "Moose to gorilla. Gorilla to final location."

Danny had backed away and stood against

the side wall of the warehouse. He looked on, amazed and confused.

He saw a robot gorilla tuck the Night Scientist under his arm and lope steadily across the warehouse before leaping up, swinging on a metal rafter and vanishing feet first through the warehouse door.

The Night Scientist's howls slowly died away.

There were a few seconds of silence. Eric was the first to speak.

"Hope he likes snow. Because he's off for a holiday in the North Pole!" he said, climbing off his rhino.

Danny gave a loud, relieved laugh, and Eric and Mia joined in.

"Now then. Who's got the remotes?" asked Uncle Charlie.

"We have," said Roxie, stepping out from behind a robot yak.

"Safe as houses," said Jasper, stepping out from behind a baboon.

"Jasper! Roxie! You're OK!" said Danny. "When I flew away – I know you told me to go – but I felt bad – I felt –"

"It's fine, Danny," said Jasper. "You did the right thing."

"We won in the end," said Roxie with a wink. "We always do."

Uncle Charlie gave Danny another hug.

"So it turns out those robot animals are really easy to rewire," said Eric. "Just like that parrot was. You and Uncle Charlie gave me enough time to reprogramme this batch. We just shut the others down."

"Wow," said Danny. "So when did you all get here? And how did you all get here? And how did you all meet up?"

"We'll give you the full story when we get home," said Uncle Charlie, "but this is my part. Till two days ago, I was stuck inside one of the

Night Scientist's giant fish. I had a mobile phone but couldn't get a signal while the fish was swimming in the open sea. I had to wait till it got close to shore, then I was able to call out. I phoned Jasper and Roxie. Jasper used the phone's signal to pinpoint my location and got me out by direct matter transfer. Trouble was, he only got me as far as Georgia, then he had to stop for a rest. By then, I was being chased by bears and Jasper lost my signal. So I had to travel the rest of the way on my own."

"OK," murmured Danny.

"Two days later, I made it to your house. I arrived about half an hour after you'd left with Jasper and Roxie. Eric and Mia told me the remote had gone and insisted on coming with me. We caught up with Jasper and Roxie when they were being attacked by those insects. We managed to bash and mangle a fair few. Of course, by that point, you'd gone."

"I know," said Danny. "I'd decided—"

"I knew exactly what you'd do!" said Uncle Charlie with a smile. "Find the man who took your remote. I'd have done the same, you see! Anyway, we all headed here as fast as we could. We must have arrived not long after you. Eric and Mia started rewiring the animals while Jasper, Roxie and I tried to track you down. We heard noises from in here, so I sent you that message to your remote. Then Jasper beamed me in. I knew Eric needed another ten minutes to finish rewiring the animals so I kept the Night Scientist talking. Then in they came."

"In you came," said Danny with a smile.

He looked down and remembered that he wasn't holding his remote. He realised that he didn't care.

"So all these animals will do what you say, Eric?" asked Danny.

"Yeah. Cool, eh?" said Eric. "I probably won't take all of them home, though. That would be ridiculous. I'll leave – maybe – those two here."

He pointed at a couple of wonky-looking geese.

"And him," he added.

He gestured towards a rabbit with smoke coming out of one of his ears.

Jasper held up the two remotes. "So how come there are two of these contraptions?" he asked.

"Tell 'em, Danny," said Uncle Charlie.

"The Night Scientist split the amber crystal and built his own one," said Danny.

So Danny told everyone about the last half an hour and how the Night Scientist's remote was even more powerful than his and how both were now programmed to respond to the Night Scientist's voice.

"Give it here, Jazza," said Uncle Charlie, taking it from Jasper.

Uncle Charlie pressed the crystal in the back of Danny's remote. He twisted it anticlockwise until it pinged.

"That'll be fine now," said Uncle Charlie. "Back to its original settings."

He handed it to Danny.

"As for this," said Uncle Charlie, picking up the Night Scientist's remote. "Mia, would you like to do the honours?"

Mia smiled, took the remote, dropped it on the floor and ground it under her heel.

"One more stamp for luck?" suggested Uncle Charlie.

Mia brought her foot down sharply and the remote fell apart.

"Now that is a real talent," said Uncle Charlie.

Danny looked round at all his friends and family. He wondered if he should press Pause and prolong this happy moment. But he didn't want to be alone; he wanted his uncle to be here with him, to be living and breathing and walking and talking beside him.

So instead he did something else. He pressed Record and watched the yellow light stream out of his remote. He moved his arm slowly from left to right, recording Eric, Mia, Uncle Charlie, Roxie, Jasper and all of the robot animals. Eric and Mia stood quietly smiling at him, their eyes bright and their faces shining. He let the stream of light rest on Uncle Charlie for a few seconds.

He persuaded Jasper and Roxie to wave. Then he moved the stream of light back from right to left, capturing everything, missing nothing, determined to record the moment as faithfully as possible.

Then he pressed Stop.

Danny and Mia were standing outside their house. Uncle Charlie was hovering behind them.

"Do we have to?" asked Danny.

Uncle Charlie nodded.

"Where do you live?" asked Mia. "We could stay with you."

Uncle Charlie shook his head.

"But tell you what, I'll come and stay with you for a while," he added.

Danny and Mia clapped their hands and laughed.

"Deal," said Mia.

"Do you think the Night Scientist will make it back from the North Pole?" said Danny as they walked towards the front door.

"If he does, Jasper and Roxie will simply escort him to the South Pole," said Uncle Charlie.

"Do you think he'll invent another remote of his own?" asked Danny.

"No. He'd need an amber crystal for that, and we'll make sure he never gets another one," said Uncle Charlie.

"And he won't have his animals any more," added Mia, "because Eric's taken them all apart."

"Except the lemur," said Uncle Charlie. "We let him keep the lemur for a week."

They were outside the front door now. Danny was holding his remote loosely in his right hand.

"Wait," he said.

"What's up?" said Uncle Charlie.

"You really don't want to face Mum and Dad, do you?" said Mia.

"No, it's not that," said Danny. "It's this."

He held out his remote.

"I don't need it right now," he said.

Uncle Charlie frowned slightly.

"I want you to look after it for a while," said Danny.

He held it out and Uncle Charlie took it gently.

Mia had a concerned look on her face. "Are you sure about this?" she asked.

Danny nodded. "It's someone else's turn," he said.

Uncle Charlie smiled and gave Danny's arm a squeeze.

"Let me tell you something about the gadgets I look after," he said. "You might have guessed the first part. That is, if we ever lend a gadget out, we make sure it's programmed so that it only recognises one person's fingerprints. See what that means? No one else can use that remote. Only you. So what's the point of giving it to someone else?"

Danny shrugged.

"But that's not all," said Uncle Charlie. "They don't work if they don't match your deepest dreams and desires."

"Eh?" said Danny and Mia at the same time.

"Each gadget is paired with someone who really *needs* it," said Uncle Charlie. "And, Danny, you *really* needed to step out of time. You didn't need rocket boots. You didn't need laser vision. You needed a cosmic remote."

"I see," said Danny. "I think."

"And when you stop needing it," said Uncle Charlie. 'It'll stop working."

"Oh," said Danny, looking slightly uncertain.

"Want to see if it still works?" said Uncle Charlie.

"Er, OK," said Danny.

He pressed Pause. Mia and Uncle Charlie froze. He pressed Play.

"It still works," said Danny.

"Then you still need it," said Uncle Charlie. "For now."

He put his arms round Danny and Mia and squeezed them tight.

"Ready to go inside?" he said.

Danny looked at Uncle Charlie and Mia

smiling at him. He felt ready for anything. He slipped his remote into his pocket and followed them into the house.

Read all about Danny's next big adventure in

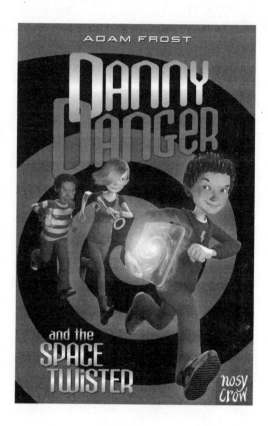